SCORING THE KEEPER

ARCTIC TITANS OF NORTHWOOD U BOOK TWO

HAYDEN HALL

Copyright © 2023 by Hayden Hall

All rights reserved.

ISBN: 979-8-8610-6356-2

No part of this book may be reproduced in any form or by any electronic or mechanical means, including information storage and retrieval systems, without written permission from the author, except for the use of brief quotations in a book review.

Cover photo by XramRagde

Cover design by Angela Haddon

Edited by Sabrina Hutchinson

Written by Hayden Hall

www.haydenhallwrites.com

 Created with Vellum

About the Book

Sawyer Price is the broodiest, most stubborn guy I ever had the joy of tutoring. He is also the sexiest, most irresistible jock at Northwood U. His hockey scholarship depends on passing the general courses and I'm the cleverest physics cog on campus.

I'm kind of brilliant. Not that I'm bragging. But the line of students in need of my help has got to mean something, right? And because I can't tutor them all, I'm forced to choose my students another way.

The thing is, no matter how smart I might be, I'm a total dating disaster. So when Sawyer and I find a mutually beneficial arrangement, I have no way out. He's going to teach me how to score a guy. And I would be mad to refuse. After all, everyone is dying to hang out with Sawyer Price.

The problem with having no dating experience whatsoever is that my tutor quickly becomes my newest obsession. But a guy like that would never want to have me for real, right? I'm just a hopeless nerd trying to trade my V-card and he's the star goalie for *Arctic Titans*.

We are polar opposites in every way. Even if we take things a step further, we can never really be together.

It seems like the final dating lesson I must learn is on the subject of heartbreak.

ONE

Sawyer

Fuck physics.

I sneered at the faculty building as I passed it, then pulled my coat closer around my body. It swallowed me whole, but I didn't mind the warmth it provided against the chilly January winds. The building was just another Gothic, brick-and-mortar monstrosity that looked eerie as fuck on a winter evening. The orange lights beaming from the recessed ground fixtures made the walls glow and didn't help much in making it look any friendlier.

Professor Wallaby made it less friendly still.

She was the bane of my hockey career. Or would be soon. Her golden curls, that defied the laws of the physics she droned on and on about, remained still and high despite the elements. Her red-framed glasses perched on the tip of her nose and accented the murder glare she could shoot over the upper frame. All because I thought Heisenberg was that guy from *Breaking Bad*. How the hell was I supposed to know some random scientist was the inspiration behind the pseudonym? They never said that in the show.

Alright. So I was dumb. But it wasn't like I planned on teaching physics when Wallaby retired. Which, admittedly, was going to be *never* anyway. The story went, she couldn't stand her husband's endless lectures on English literature day in and day out, so she remained a full time professor well into her retirement years.

All I needed was a passing grade. And yet, after spending an entire afternoon in the library, I was no closer to it than I had been three months ago. So I made my way through crusty snow back to the neo-colonial house that my team called our home.

Northwood's campus was a massive plot of land that pretty much declared independence. It was never quiet. Students milled about every which way I looked. And unless they were looking to go clubbing all night, nobody needed to leave the premises. Ever. In its inner ring was the student center with every possible amenity one could need. Reading rooms, coworking spaces, a library, a bookstore, cafes, restaurants, bars, and a twenty-four-seven gym all nestled in the center. And around it, occupying space in every direction, were faculty buildings and administration facilities. Beyond those, there were sports facilities for Northwood's greatest point of pride, the *Arctic Titans*, as well as the clumsy baseball bat swingers and the football giants. An Olympic pool was the outermost building in the athletic sector. On the opposite end were sprawling dormitories, fraternity and sorority houses, and team houses, such as ours.

It felt like coming home, especially when I stomped my feet at the door to rid myself of the snow on my *Doc Martens* and entered the warm common room on the ground floor. I made my way straight to the basement where the real common room was. I didn't bother pulling my earbuds out. *Killing in the Name* by Rage Against the Machine played at maximum volume, drowning out everything else. The basement was fairly empty with all the parties on campus keeping the frat bros warm and occupied. Riley and Cameron were on the far sofa, playing their nerdy game, and Sebastian and Avery were rocking the soccer table in a fierce battle.

I nodded at them all when heads turned and greetings were said. My anger was such that speaking at all risked me lashing out and I reined that in as much as I could. Instead, I marched to the fridge and grabbed a can of beer, then plopped down into an armchair far from anyone else for a few moments of venting. My playlist moved on and AC/DC's *Back in Black* filled my skull with its good old-fashioned hard rock.

I sipped my beer and closed my eyes until a hand touched my shoulder. I looked up.

Avery stood still, waiting. His eyebrows were in a flat line over his gray eyes, his lips pressed together appeared even sharper than they naturally were.

I pulled one earbud out and held it two inches away from my ear. The song was nearing the best part. "Huh?"

"Who do I need to kick in the balls?" he asked.

"That crone Wallaby," I muttered.

"Tsk." Avery lowered himself to the very edge of the other armchair, spread his legs wide, and set his elbows on his knees. He shook his head. "That'll be complicated."

"You think? Unless you're flunking biology, you shouldn't even try going after her balls." I brought the can to my lips and swigged more beer. It tickled my mouth and left a bitter aftertaste. As if I needed more reasons to snarl.

Avery blinked, which was his equivalent to laughing his ass off. "Have you talked to her?"

"This morning," I said. And when he was silent, I proceeded to tell him, and all the others in the basement, how that had gone down. Basically, Wallaby had invited me into her office to tell me I needed to get my act together. The overdue papers last semester had been half the reason I had failed. In her words, it was lucky that she was offering the same course this semester, so I could retake it and earn my credits, but I needed to "Start putting in the bare minimum, Mister Price," I shrilled in Wallaby's voice.

"Okay, that's a shit impression. Don't do that again." Avery remained deadpan.

"About that ball-kicking?" I reminded him. "Do your own, asshole."

"I'll pass. So, what happened next?" He folded his hands together and held my gaze without blinking.

I snorted. "What happened next? 'Yes, Ma'am. Of course, Ma'am.' And I was out."

"She didn't tell you how to actually put that bare minimum in, huh?" Avery asked.

I shook my head, pulling the other earbud out because I had totally lost my concentration. "I guess there's no hope for me at all, boys."

"There is." Avery was short and to the point as ever. "You fail again, you take the summer session. There are options."

"Seriously, dude. If I fail twice, the summer session will be a nice epilogue that changes nothing." As I said this, Riley twisted on the sofa to face me better.

"Have you tried getting in touch with Noah?" he asked.

I let out a strangled laugh. "Have I tried? Everyone I talked to said he was booked until the twenty-fourth century. People are literally scheduling which courses they expect to fail before they're even admitted, then getting in touch with him. I got as far as talking to Matt Hughes, Noah's best friend. And he told me I was way too late. Besides, Noah's coaching nerds for competitions most of the time."

"Did you actually see the guy?" Riley asked.

"Do you know how to make him see me?" I returned flatly.

"You're doing the thing, buddy," Avery said.

"What thing?" I snapped.

"You're being a dick. Cap's just trying to help."

I rolled my eyes and nodded. "I'm sorry, Riley. I'm just on edge."

Our team captain waved his hand off and shook his head. "It's fine. But...is it really that hard to even meet with the guy?"

I blew out a breath of air. Noah Foster was the wunderkind of physics. "Dude's won the Physics Olympiad when he was fourteen. And he's weird. You can't just go up to his room. He'll ban you for life, man."

They all laughed, Avery's laughter being a short exhale, like I was kidding.

I gawked at them. "I'm serious. Brad, the *Breakers'* goalie, tried it and Noah told him he would never, ever even hint at something that could help him get a single point he didn't earn himself. And when Brad shits himself with fear, you know the guy isn't joking. I guess it's got something to do with knocking on his door and breaking his concentration. Brad didn't know what to call it."

"Traitor," Avery accused me and I ignored him. I was desperate and I'd heard from a mutual connection that our biggest rival's goalie had met with my last resort tutor. I'd touched bases with Brad. Sue me.

"Alright," Riley said. "So, you can't go up to his room and knock because he'll blacklist you. No one you spoke with can get you in touch with him. How do you get him to tutor you, then?"

"I don't," I said.

"There must be someone else," Sebastian offered.

"Not gonna work. Sawyer scored a grand total of nothing the entire semester. He's starting from scratch." Avery was thinking aloud and I narrowed my eyes at him.

"Thanks, buddy," I said.

He ignored me. "We need Noah. He's the only one who could, in theory, do this. We're talking about teaching a toddler how to build a rocket."

"Thanks some more, buddy." I exhaled and slid lower in my seat until my ass was practically hanging over the edge. The can rested on my chest, my hands wrapped around it, elbows cozy on the armrests.

"He's gotta have a price," Avery said ultimately.

"He's already expensive as all fuck," I pointed out. Still, it was cheaper than losing my scholarship and getting kicked off the team. My entire career was hanging on by a thread.

"Nah, that's not what I meant," Avery said. "He's coaching nerds for competitions, but isn't competing himself, huh? Weird. But why is he tutoring them? What does he get from them winning a competition? Glory? Favors? Connections? He must have a reason."

I groaned as loudly as I could. This was driving me fucking insane.

"What if he's just weird and wants to flex?" Cameron asked with a serious expression on his face.

"What if he's tutoring those that will go on to make a difference?" Sebastian offered.

"None of that is helpful," Riley said flatly.

Avery was opening his mouth when I put my earbuds back in and set the can on the small table in front of me. "Fuck this. Fuck everything. Fuck Noah. I'm going to that frat party." And with that, I was out of the basement and marching to the party that was a few blocks away from our house.

This entire week had been hell and it was only the first of the semester. My body was already bruised from hockey drills and a few clumsy pucks slamming into my leg and arm. My brain was fried and I hadn't even started studying. My hopes had evaporated after a short relief of being back home with my family. "I know you'll work it out, buddy," Dad had told me on my way back here. "Even if it looks hopeless, don't give up just yet."

And that was what really made my heartstrings quiver. They'd put so much trust in me, Mom and Dad. They'd cheered me on at every turn and hoped for the best no matter what my endeavors were. When I inevitably failed and returned home with my tail between my legs, they wouldn't let their disappointment show. Oh no. Nobody would raise a voice or even say I could have done better. In their eyes, I was already doing the best job ever. They would nod and pat my shoulder, then tell me how awesome I was for all the effort I'd put in.

Goddammit.

I sighed and stomped the snow off at the entrance to the frat house. They were blasting party music on a surround system that made the roof jump off the house.

The beats were steady, but the melody was bland and the autotuned vocals were forming lazy thoughts through easily memorized lines. There was nothing inspiring about it. Then again, I was here to lose myself in the crowd and maybe get laid. I wasn't exactly looking for music that would make me transcend dimensions.

The party-goers were still in the early stages of getting into it. Frat bros and sorority girls mingled awkwardly, feigning disinterest and boredom in this weird, contemporary way of flirting. Everyone was putting a lot of effort into pretending they weren't into you. And who was better at that than me?

I sent a few nods here and there that substituted a 'Sup?' which took too much effort by today's standards. Just the earrings that dangled from my ears and the uninterested look I shot to everyone were enough to get me noticed. Add to that the abundance of line art tattoos that snaked from beneath my clothes, licking along my neck and the backs of my hands, as well as the fact I was the *Titans*' goalie, and that was it. Two sophomore brunettes sent me looks I didn't return and a blond chick with a pierced nose offered me a drink, which I took. What I lacked in height and mass, I made up for in definition and aesthetic. As a goalie, I was the unusual one, but nobody was as fast as me. What I lacked in size before the goal post, I made up for in my skill.

It was going to be such a shame when all of that skill went to waste because I lost my scholarship. Oh well. At least the drink was biting my throat and burning on the way down. That would help me weather the night. I only had so many left until the end of May.

"I've seen you around," the blond said.

"Oh yeah?" I didn't look at her. Those were the flirting rules.

"Heather, is this guy bothering you?" a deep voice interrupted just as Heather inhaled to say that yeah, she totally had seen me around.

"Back off, Zach," Heather said.

"Seems like *you're* bothering her," I pointed out, still looking straight, leaning against the wall. "And she can take care of herself."

"That she can," Heather said and pushed Zach hard enough to send the message. I didn't know either of them, but the girl was growing on me. "Sorry about that loser."

"Not your fault," I said, struggling to get in a good mood for anything more than chitchat.

"It actually is," Heather said. "He's my twin brother. He probably thinks he was flirting with you."

I looked at her, then at Zach, and back at her. Yep. They were siblings. Same shade of blond and the same blue eyes, similar lips, and upturned noses. He was obviously a gym rat or a football jock. He glared at me, then turned away. My eyes lingered on his physique for a few moments. He had all the things I didn't, but I wondered if they served him well. The size of his bulky, chiseled torso probably slowed him down. Oh, he was lickable as fuck, but I was measuring him as a goalie. He'd keep that goalpost filled for sure, but he would have a hard time doing anything flashy.

Flashy moves were why the crowds loved me. *The Broody Bugs Bunny of Ice Hockey*, an editorial once called me. They weren't wrong.

"Honey, you're staring at my brother," Heather said softly.

I couldn't help but chuckle. "Was I?"

"I'm jealous," she said.

We caught each other's glances and exchanged a smirk. "Don't be," I said. I thrust my hand out for a shake and shook hers as I introduced myself. "Blazing bisexual. Pleased to meet you."

Heather chuckled back and shook her head. "Prancing pansexual. Pleasure's all mine."

I threw my head back and laughed out loud. "I like your style."

"You're stylish yourself," she said.

A thought crossed my mind and I hid the way it made the corners of my mouth quiver by taking another sip of my drink. Whatever the hell she had given me was vodka based. I didn't care to find out the rest. What I cared about was Heather. Tonight. Then, if the stars aligned, Zach. Wouldn't that make it a bingo?

And as Heather began asking about my tattoos, I glanced back at Zach who was melting into the crowd. He looked over his shoulder and found me whispering something back to Heather, our gazes lingering on one another for a few moments. He rolled his eyes and turned away.

This was going to be a fun game to play. And when Heather caught me glancing at her twin, she gave a coy smile that said she was interested in exactly the same amount of attachment as I was. Could I give her a night to remember? Hell yeah. And would she give a damn who I went after the next day? Not in a million years.

For a moment, I could stop thinking about Wallaby and physics and the impossibility of finding Noah Foster. For a night, I could indulge in the thrill of the chase.

Oh yeah. The game was on.

TWO

Noah

"Everyone here is rude, Matt." I fixed my glasses and ran a hand through my unruly hair. Each time the beat dropped, my stomach rose. I was going to be sick just from the smell of sweat and spilled beer. I didn't need the bass rocking my body this hard on top of everything else.

"They're not rude," Matt said, holding two plastic cups, red on the outside, white on the inside, and filled with the golden liquid I had no taste for. "That's what people are like."

"People are rude," I insisted.

"And you're never going to meet anyone if you don't give them a chance." He gave me a pointed look.

"Maybe I don't want to meet anyone," I said sulkily. "Maybe I'm enough for myself."

"You, my darling, are a handful for anyone, but a date wouldn't kill you." He took a sip of his beer and looked like he had just knocked on the Pearly Gates.

I sniffed the air and cringed. "What's that smell? Are someone's socks on fire?"

Matt inhaled deeply and looked positively pleased. "That, my friend, means there's a working bong in this house. Laters." He thrust the beer into my hand and winked, then disappeared into the crowd.

I was shit at parties. No, actually, I was shit with people. Parties without people were totally fine. And this particular party was packed with pretty much every type of person my personality clashed with.

If only I could be more like Matt, who was a rare human I wasn't terrified of. He could just walk up to anyone and blend in. There was no doubt in my mind that the bong users had no idea who Matt was, but when he approached them, he would be welcome. And good for him. I just wished he would make good on his word to be my wingman.

I was half-certain he had given up on me ever actually scoring a date. The last million attempts he'd made had ended in me stammering, offering an obscure piece of comic book trivia, snorting at my own physics joke, and the other guy yawning in my face.

I looked around the spacious ground floor area of the neo-colonial frat house, parsing through people I'd seen before. All alone, I had no choice but to pick a human and approach him. He was a frat bro by the look of him, partying in his sweatpants and hoodie, currently all by himself because the two other guys began making out and moved a few feet to the side. He wasn't that much bigger than me, which made him less scary, but he was still as far out of my comfort zone as I could push myself.

I missed my striped pajamas and soft slippers.

"Hey," I said, curling my toes in my shoes like I was grounding myself.

The frat bro scanned me and I watched interest leave his face. "'Sup?" His head was turning away as he spoke.

"Not much," I sighed and blended back into the wall. He never noticed.

I wasn't exactly the Hunchback of Notre Dame, but I wasn't your sexy fuckboy, either. My only strength was my sharp brain and that brought my average up. But being smart about stuff and knowing how to do stuff were two things that I had never reconciled in my life. And for some reason, I had been stupid enough to believe that focusing on my mental capacity would make me happy. Silly me. Why on Earth would I have believed that?

Oh yeah. Mom and Dad, I thought sarcastically. Not that I should blame them for making me into a socially inept, awkward, and introverted geek. Which wasn't to say I didn't blame them anyway.

I kept looking around the house. Here, a girl was tripping over her own feet. There, a guy was glaring at another, more distant guy who was smiling and joking with a blond girl. What the hell was all that about? And further still, Matt was red-eyed and holding the most blissful little smile of contentment that I ever did see. He spotted me, then made his way toward me. "Get laid yet?" he asked as he reached me.

I rolled my eyes and covered up my blush by drinking tiny sips of beer for a long while. If anything, it cooled me down. Not that Matt knew how well his arrow had struck the bullseye. Even my best of friends wasn't included in that bombshell. "Do I look like I got laid?"

Matt narrowed his eyes at me and considered me for a time. "Laid? No. You look like you got screwed. What happened?"

"Everyone. At. This. Party. Is. Rude." I finished my beer and felt like I needed to burp. *Oh no. Oh, God. Not here among people. What do I do?* I held my breath and looked around, waiting for it to settle. If I accidentally belched in a crowd, I might as well climb the highest level of this house and put Newton's laws of gravity to the test.

Matt, however, finished his beer and roared a rift shamelessly, then wrinkled his nose when several people laughed. "Not my finest hour, I'll admit it," he said.

I wanted the ground to open under my feet and swallow me whole.

"I used to be able to belch through half the alphabet," he bragged.

"Try that the next time you're pulled over," I teased. He'd been pulled over with me in the car and the officer was the most stunning young woman I'd ever seen. Obviously, she left Matt tongue-tied at once, which firmly assured her that he was drunk. He'd recited the alphabet backward and walked in a straight line, then ended up blowing the balloon until it was proved, beyond a shred of doubt, that he was not drunk, but merely an idiot.

"It happened once, dammit." Matt slapped my shoulder and shook it a little. "I still dream of her." His tone was soft and dreamy and way over the top. And when he began giggling, I remembered he'd been testing that bong.

"How about we head back?" I asked.

"Are you mad? The party's barely started," he said. "And my mission is to score you a date for the next one."

"You're basically giving me up for adoption is what I hear." I deadpanned and Matt stretched his lips into a huge grin and looked into my eyes. He ran a hand through my hair, straightened my little bowtie, told me to exhale, sniffed, then patted my shoulders. "Minty breath, clean fingernails, nice hair. There's no mother who wouldn't want you as her son-in-law."

"I'm not exactly trying to score someone's mom," I said.

"That's as close to a yo-mama joke you'll ever get, my friend," Matt said, feigning heartbreaking disappointment, then sliding his arm over my shoulders and looking around. "How about that guy?"

I looked at where he was pointing. "Are you fucking crazy?" I asked.

"Language, Mister," Matt said. "And what's wrong with him?"

The guy Matt was still pointing at very visibly, was a six-foot-four boulder of muscles, a drop-dead gorgeous face, upturned nose, blue eyes, and bright blond hair. He was an all-American beauty. He was a walking stock photo that advertised anything from Greek Life to college football or sexy cologne. "He's slightly out of my league. Stop pointing your finger at him." I swatted Matt's hand down and exhaled in frustration. The blond guy was making his way to the one that had been hanging out with the blond girl. The girl had gone somewhere and the two guys struck up a conversation. "This is stupid. I really just want to go."

Matt raised his hands in surrender. "Alright. I'm not gonna force you."

I felt bad instantly. Matt had been trying to help me solve my single biggest problem ever and he didn't even know what the problem was. He had no clue about my lack of experience. And not just in dating and networking, but in everything. He just assumed there was an app that took care of the awkward bit and got me action, but he couldn't be more wrong. Yeah, I'd downloaded apps at one point, and they had freaked me out so much and so quickly that I'd never opened them again.

He had no idea I was a virgin. And every day that passed, I was a virgin for a day longer, which made it harder to tackle that monolithic *first time*.

"If you want, we can go," Matt said. And he meant it, but I couldn't do that to him.

"I'm good," I said bravely. "You can have fun and I'll stick around." Matt moved away to mingle with the crowd.

There was pizza in boxes all over the place, so I grabbed a slice, decidedly not worrying about who else had touched it. It made me think of my personal hero, Nikola Tesla, who was such a germaphobe that he supposedly stopped shaking people's hands. His solitary life was on the list of things I had in common with the great man. And, according to some whispers and unproven gossip, remaining a virgin was on the same list. *And none of that made him any less brilliant*, I told myself as I went down a mental rabbit hole of considering Tesla's achievements and life. He had immigrated to the US to work for Thomas Edison on the promise of a huge payment if he could improve Edison's direct current. And when he did, Edison claimed the payment promise had been a joke all along. It was only the first of many slights and still, at least today, Tesla's genius was getting the appropriate appreciation.

Did you ever stop to consider that thinking about Nikola Tesla at a frat party might be why you're still a virgin? The snarky voice inside my head was right, but I indulged anyway. I chewed my pizza and washed it down with sparkling, sour, and bitter beer. It was a horrible combination and my time would have been better spent doing literally anything else. I could have been reviewing my notes from senior year's introduction to astrophysics. I had a session with a student who was two years ahead of me, but I'd already covered the grounds privately. In high school.

I sighed and looked to the other side of the crowded area. Some sort of commotion was taking place over there around the black-haired, tattooed, broody guy who looked ever so slightly amused. The blond girl and the jock Matt had been pointing at were starting to debate something loudly while, between them, the black-haired boy crossed his arms over his chest and nodded at everything.

But the debate grew heated quickly and the black-haired hottie was starting to seem surprised. He was, without a doubt, the best looking, most confident specimen of a college fuckboy I had ever seen. The dangling earrings, the pouty lips, the bored expression. If you took everyone at this party's best features and combined them all together, it would make *him*. His dark, slanting eyes and the tattoos rising along his neck made me short of breath.

The hot guy was raising his hands when the two blonds looked at him for answers. The girl grabbed his upper arm and yanked him towards her, but the guy was also doing the same thing, almost spilling the drink the hottie was holding in the process. As I watched, Matt came closer to me. "See? That guy's gay. You could have struck up a conversation with him and seen where it went."

"And do you see that he's into the other guy?" I asked.

"That's Sawyer." Matt said, his tone holding no surprise. "What the hell is happening over there anyway?"

Sawyer, apparently, was everything I was not. Even as he was being torn apart by two blonds, he seemed as confident as if there was nothing the other two wanted but him. And by the look of it, there wasn't. They were pulling him back and forth, hotly telling each other to back off. "You know him?" I asked Matt.

"Yeah, he was asking how to get in touch with you," Matt said casually as if brushing it off while focusing on the brewing fight over there.

My heart tripped and I took a moment to sort through my thoughts. This hot as hell guy wanted to get in touch with me? He knew of me? But, as my brain sped up, I remembered the only reason anyone ever wanted to get in touch with me. I deadpanned at Matt. "To tutor him?"

"Obviously. You don't go seducing twins and acing courses. And Sawyer's the type who loves to seduce." Matt was all distant, frowning at the commotion. "Don't worry. I told him you were booked."

He could say that again. I was booked for the rest of the year and had more than a few students vowing to need my help next year, too, sending me preliminary times and dates together with boxes of chocolate.

Of course a guy like Sawyer needed my help. If he didn't, he wouldn't notice me even if he tripped over me. I'd been shoved into my locker by guys like him my entire life. It didn't make me crave them any less, but it did adjust my expectations.

"An athlete?" I asked. He sort of looked like a baseball player. Maybe. I didn't know much about baseball.

"Hockey," Matt said. "He's the *Titans'* goalie."

"A keeper," I mused, looking at the two people he'd charmed fighting over him.

"I was here first," the girl was shouting.

"Yeah, but maybe we should let him choose," the guy insisted.

"He already chose. Didn't you, Sawyer?" the girl pressed.

"Don't involve me." Sawyer was shaking his hands and head, careful not to spill his nearly full plastic cup of whatever he was drinking. "I'll go either way."

I snort-laughed because I'd expected him to say he didn't want anything to do with the fight. But the fucker was fanning the flames and loving every moment of it.

The crowd dispersed slightly and I found myself pushing closer to the three squabbling lovebirds, Matt on my heels. And just as I tried to seem less like I was staring, the fight went nuclear.

"He's been making eye contact with me all night," the big guy was saying. I wouldn't have minded making eye contact with him all night, too, if I were in Sawyer's shoes. But he seemed equally enthralled with the girl, too.

"And we've been chatting all night, asshole," the girl was saying. "You're ruining everything, Zach. And if you're so desperate to get a piece of him, then wait your goddamn turn."

"I'm not taking your sloppy seconds, Sis," the guy snarled. And as it got heated, Sawyer lifted his cute, straight eyebrows and turned around as if to sneak out of the way. I couldn't see his face now that his back was turned to me. But just as he was fully facing away from me, the girl grabbed his wrist, and the guy, Zach, grabbed his shoulder. They insisted something into his ear from each side and Sawyer jerked back, his arm suddenly free of the girl's hold. It shot up, together with the plastic cup he was holding, and slammed against his shoulder.

Newton's First Law played out in real time as the contents of Sawyer's cup were in motion and remained in motion even when the cup stopped abruptly. The liquid — vodka with orange juice, I soon discovered — crossed the distance between us in an instant and splashed all over my face, glasses, shirt, and bowtie, soaking my hair and making me gape.

"Fuck," Sawyer said, spinning around from the two siblings who stopped fighting the moment there was collateral damage.

I blinked twice, dripping with booze and smelling like orange juice. "Um..."

Sawyer moved his gaze from me to my companion. "Matt? Is this...?" As his gaze returned to me, it grew ten times more horrified as he recognized me. "Oh, no. Oh, shit."

I licked my lips. "I think I'll head back now." Using my sleeve, I wiped some of the vodka-juice off my face to no point or purpose and cut through the crowd toward the door.

"Noah, wait," Sawyer said, but I was already so embarrassed that my cheeks couldn't get any redder. As the shame mixed with the terrifying fear of being in the spotlight — as I very much was — I barely knew what I was doing. I raced out of the frat house, telling myself that I had known all along that a party was a terrible idea.

I ran faster, losing breath soon enough, then slowing down. Dormitories were lined up on the northern part of campus, only a little distant from the houses that fraternities and athletes had. And mine, a long, two-story building, was the closest. I rushed in and up the stairs, then down the first floor hallway until I reached the last door on the right. I barged in as soon as the key turned in the lock, then slammed the door shut and released a deep exhale. *Fucking fuck*. There were many ways to embarrass me, for sure, but none were as effective as the public splashing of a beverage onto my face. And that goddamn, puck-loving, ice-skating, physics-failing asshole did just that in a house that packed half our campus. By morning, everyone would know about it. And everyone would laugh at me behind my back.

I was so screwed.

I needed to transfer to another college. Preferably another state. Or maybe to Germany. That sounded nice and far enough. And, ideally, I would pull that off before sunrise.

After I showered the stink of juice and booze and other people's sweat off my body, I pulled on my black boxer-briefs with eggplants printed all over them as some charm to attract, er, eggplants.

Back in my room, I slipped under the comforter and lifted a copy of *Principles of Stellar Evolution and Nucleosynthesis* that I'd found in the library a few days earlier. The room was warm, but the heat of embarrassment was warmer. It radiated out of me. It tugged on my attention in every way. There was no reading tonight.

I dropped the textbook and looked around. It was Friday. It was night. The campus was buzzing with people falling in love, having sex, vomiting, eating junk food at odd hours, and living their lives to the fullest. And here I was, lying in my bed.

It was a good bed. Winning a Physics Olympiad guaranteed a lot of perks. Scholarship, a spacious dorm room all to myself, access to all physics teachers at any time of the day because they wished to network and shape me. It also guaranteed a nice income from tutoring, especially when I realized that demand was such that I could choose my own students. So I chose the best of the best. Gone were the days of tutoring football jocks in exchange for protection like I'd had to do in high school. Little good did that do.

My room was a cozy place. In fact, it was the coziest place I'd ever lived in. Its walls were a dark cream, the closet and bookshelves matched the same type of wood and shade of brown, and the rug was a dark red over the deep brown hardwood floor. The desk was slightly off in tone, a lighter shade of brown than all else, with a black office chair screwing up my *feng shui*. Lamps were my main source of light, although there were lights on the ceiling, too. The bed was bigger than the one I'd had at home, where my parents had designed a room with a lot of workspace and little comfort. My trophies from local, state, and national level science fairs and physics competitions dotted a shelf above my bed. Rocket models and spaceships added soul to the same shelf. Posters of alien worlds in all their retro sci-fi glory featured *Foundation's* Terminus and *Dune's* Arrakis, as well as a few others that weren't based on any existing intellectual property, but were simply an artist's ideas of what a gas giant's surface would look like.

Above my bed, a string of dim white Christmas lights stretched under the bookshelf, over another poster — this one was of *Babylon 5* — and down to the outlet behind my nightstand.

I closed my eyes and dropped my glasses on the nightstand, then sank into the big, soft pillow and exhaled with a groan.

As I did, I realized several things at once. It was lucky beyond belief that Matt had turned Sawyer away for me. I had no time and no use in that endeavor. However, at the same time, I found myself imagining sitting next to him, our knees touching by accident, his long locks of hair falling over his face as he followed the equations I was explaining.

He really was a breathtaking one. The tattoos, the earrings, the piercing in his left nostril, and those gorgeous, half-moon eyes.

This is why it's lucky Matt put a stop to it, I thought. I would never be able to concentrate and neither of us would get anything out of those sessions. I would secretly drool over him and make blunders while stammering my explanations for his problems. He would learn nothing. A talented physics student would have less chance of success because I wouldn't direct my time and attention to them. And that was the end of it.

No matter the delicious eye candy that Sawyer was, he would be a horrible waste of my time. Besides, he'd made me into the biggest loser and gossip on campus tonight.

I would be smart to keep reminding myself of that.

THREE

Sawyer

I HAPPENED TO BE IN THE LIBRARY ON SATURDAY morning. There was nothing suspicious about a college student spending time in the campus library. Sure, I would normally be on a treadmill at this time, but I had a hunch that the time when the jocks filled the gym, nerds might flock to the reading rooms.

And it just so happens that I was looking for some physics textbooks to teach myself the basics. I had every reason to be here and at this time. Just because I was also looking for a shaggy-haired guy wearing a shirt, suspenders, and a bowtie, it didn't make me a stalker, right?

So when Noah Foster passed by me wearing a baggy hoodie and a pair of oversized sweatpants that swallowed his figure, I almost didn't recognize him. Luckily, he recognized me.

Or, unluckily, to be more precise.

As he passed by me, his bright green gaze sharpened and he all but growled at me. It was so intense that I nearly stepped back between two massive bookshelves. I quickly compared this guy to the version I had seen last night. He'd looked like a nerd, but at least he'd had a shape. Not that he looked bad, exactly. He still had that casual, pillow-combed hairdo going on and his face was handsome, but he was easy to miss with all these clothes hanging off his body.

"Hey, dude," I greeted him, having to turn on my heels and follow him because he picked up his pace as he spotted me. I quickly pulled my earbuds out and cut off Ozzy Osborne's voice so I could hear Noah.

I shouldn't have bothered because Noah said nothing.

"Er, I said 'hello.'" I caught up with him and marched down the hall of bookshelves shoulder to shoulder with the king of geeks.

"And I didn't," he replied. "Goodbye."

It caught me so off guard that I literally stopped in my tracks for a moment, frowning and trying to figure out what just happened.

Noah turned left and disappeared between some bookcases, but I hurried and caught up with him again. "That was kinda rude," I pointed out and, I swear to God, I wished I had bitten my damn tongue off instead.

Noah rounded on me. "Are you kidding me? That was rude? The entire campus is laughing their asses off because a nerd got drenched in vodka last night. They're saying this is the most booze I have ever had in my life."

I blinked twice, gobsmacked into silence. "But...is it true?" I stretched my lips into the faintest smile I could manage.

Noah narrowed his eyes at me like he could slice me in half with the sheer power of his look. "It's not...exactly. I don't drink. Sue me."

He moved his foot to my left and I appeared in front of him, blocking his way. I exhaled. "Listen, I'm sorry about the drink. I'll take full responsibility. Even though it was barely my fault. It was more like I was the catapult that other people operated. You can't blame the catapult when it works, right?"

"Sorry, was this an apology?" He cocked his head, his glasses catching a twinkle of the yellow ceiling light. His cheeks turned ever so slightly pink and his lips were stuck in a permanent thin line of anger.

We were nearly the same height, though I was broader and maybe an inch taller. And maybe it was my *Doc Martens* that gave me the slight advantage of looking down. Still, I needed to slouch apologetically. "You're right. I wasn't looking. Honest to God, I didn't mean to spill my drink all over you. I didn't even know who you were."

"And if I was someone else, would you be apologizing?" Noah's tone was flat and tight.

I balked from him and frowned. It was a good question. "I...yeah, I would have." I would have apologized right away had I had the chance.

"Because here's what I think. You came here to run into me so you could apologize and sweet-talk me into helping you with your physics course." He crossed his arms over his chest and the baggy sleeves of his hoodie pulled around his biceps. There was some shape to him after all, but he was determined to hide it.

I hadn't gotten a good look at him last night to know for sure, but I had a vague recollection of some definition beneath the well-fitted shirt and pants. Not that it mattered. That wasn't my priority. My brain was under-fucked by squabbling siblings, neither of which ended up inviting me to their room, and I had been too horrified at splashing vodka into my last shot's face to take care of business myself. But being low-key horny while pleading for mercy wasn't exactly the finest combination. "How do you know I'm failing physics? Is that public knowledge?"

Noah snorted with a truckload of contempt. "You're all the same. I know you're failing because you're standing here and you're talking to me. And now, you're going to fail for sure because I'm walking away." He bumped into me just as I blocked his passage again. "Move," he demanded.

"Talk to me," I said.

"We're done talking. I believe Matt told you I'm not taking on any more students." He pressed his hand against my chest and sucked in a breath of air, then attempted to push me. It failed, but he reddened nonetheless.

"Yeah, your pimp wouldn't let me speak to you," I said, pulling on my bitch face and deciding to risk it. Pleading wasn't going to make him change his mind. All I could do was lay it all out there in the open.

"Matt's my friend," Noah said, pulling his hand back from my hard pecs.

"I'm sure he is, but this isn't about him. I need your help, Noah. It's just like you said. I'm going to fail for sure and it'll be the end of my hockey career. I'll have to go back to some community college and settle for collecting hockey cards. If you know anything about me — and, let's face it, who doesn't? — you know I'm born to be on the ice. You know I have a promising future just like you do in…physics." Shit. What did physics majors do? Teach it to other future teachers? "Wallaby won't let me pass. She hates my guts and I need to be way better than my maximum capacity allows in order to get a mere passing grade. And that's the truth of it. So yeah, I'm talking to you now because you're my lifeline."

"There you have it," Noah said. "The story of my life."

I narrowed my eyes and cocked my head. "You're probably right. Chances are, I wouldn't be talking to you here if I didn't need you. But that's not because I'm too popular. Not just that, at least. You're a scary motherfucker, Noah."

A frown exploded over his face.

"It's a term of endearment," I explained.

"Nice fucking endearment." He was pulling back a little, looking for exit routes. I'd pressed a button there and he needed to escape me.

Oh well. I would kiss my career goodbye. "You are, though. You're the Olympiad prodigy, buddy. You have a bouncer to deal with all the students who want your help. You'll probably end up developing cloud cities on Venus or discover some particle or whatever. And if you don't think that scares people, you've got a lot to learn. And like that isn't enough, you're painting a picture of my pathetic future after I drop out because you denied me help. You're a little psycho."

His mouth dropped open and his eyes widened. "What the hell do you think you're doing?"

I had nothing else to lose. "I'm telling you what I think," I said. "Because I'll drop out in a few months anyway. So there you go."

Silence fell between us and I felt like I wanted to squirm out of my skin. I wasn't letting him leave until he said something, but I didn't know what I wanted to hear, anyway. We stared at each other until something softened in his eyes. "I...I'm really busy."

There was the slightest note of regret in his voice at having to say this. I could work with that. I could cling to that glimmer of hope. "Okay, but what if I was a super low responsibility?" I asked. "What if we made it so that you help me just a little? Something that won't make you busier?"

"I...don't know," he said. He was reluctant as fuck, but I had my foot in the door and wasn't backing off. This was how much I loved hockey. This was how much I wanted to remain on the ice, in the thick of it, in the heat of battle and the swelling pride and camaraderie of our team. "I'd have to look at my schedule."

"What if a student disappeared?" I asked, thinking I was being witty.

Noah deadpanned and rolled his eyes. "Be serious for a hot minute. I'm trying to think and you're making it impossible."

I made a little move toward him, closing the short distance between us. "I'll do anything. You're pricey as hell so I can't compete that way, but I'll do whatever the hell you want me to do."

"What do you mean?" he asked, his voice quivering.

"I dunno. You tell me. I'll be your personal servant if you need one so that you can have more time. I can bring you books from the library so you don't waste hours you could otherwise use tutoring me. I can wash your dishes, I can clean your room. I can make your weekly schedules to make sure you're using your time in the most efficient way." I was way too eager and he kept frowning at it.

"No offense, but I don't exactly trust you to be in charge of my entire life," he said, resting his fingers on my shoulders and pushing me back a little. "I saw how you handled yourself last night. You're not really the example of positive virtues."

"I'm a flirt. That's what I do. But that's only on Fridays and Saturdays. Don't you worry. I can do all of these things. And I'll get you tickets for all my hockey games if you want to watch. Front row, too. You get to see all the body checks up close."

I kept closing the distance and he kept walking back, pushing my shoulders, and walking back some more until he bumped into the bookcase and shook his head. "I don't need help with any of that. And I definitely don't need your hockey tickets."

"What, then?" I asked. "Is there anything I can do for you that'll make it worth your time? I'm desperate, man. I'm ready to whore myself out and scrub your fireplace like Cinderella if you say yes."

He blinked rapidly, then licked his lips. "There's one…I…maybe…I think I could use…if you'd…"

"Yes?" I was practically leaning against him at this point, eyes wide and pleading. We were close to a 'maybe' and it was the best feeling I have had in months. "Just say it and I'll do it."

He stammered a little more, then inhaled a deep breath of air. "How do you do it?" he all but whispered.

"Do what?" I would tell him all my secrets if he said he'd help me.

"How'd you get both of them interested last night?" he asked.

I frowned a little as I processed this. "Oh, the twins? I mean, it's what I do. It's like a hobby. You know how some people hunt animals? It's like that."

His eyebrows flattened over his rectangular, black-framed glasses and his face lost all expression. "So what? You took aim and fired a shot?"

"Sort of. Why do you ask?" My ears were ringing with confusion and my face was getting heated with the thrill of negotiation.

"Um…" He looked away. "I'm…not good…at that. Erm. Meeting people. Talking."

"Yeah, no shit." *Keep your fucking mouth shut, Price.*

Noah practically snarled at me. "Do you want my help or not?"

"I do. I swear. I'll shut up. Go on." I zipped my lips up and stepped back to give him some breathing room.

He dusted off his baggy sweater and nodded. "I suck at flirting with people. So. If you, um, want my help, you'll have to help me, too."

I swallowed and nodded vehemently. "Totally."

His eyes went wide like an owl's. "Really?"

"Oh, for sure. By the time I'm done with you, you'll be Casanova," I promised grandly. It didn't matter that I had no clue how I did what I did or how I'd ever teach him. He was more than capable of debating me at length with brittle words, but the moment he needed to mention flirting, he was an unintelligible mess. I guess it had its charms, but I wasn't sure who he would impress with that. Still, I wasn't going to debate it with him now. "Trust me, I'll make you a magnet for girls. Yeah, I know, magnets don't work like that, but pretend that girls are made of metal and it makes sense. Not Heather, though. She's fun but maybe a little too much for a beginner. We'll start simple and work from there."

"I…" He was doing the thing again. "Er, I mean, I'm not…girls…" He inhaled and exhaled, then looked into my eyes. "I'm not interested in girls."

For a moment, it felt like the threads of reality had unspooled and the universe needed to reassemble itself all over again. When it was back together, something about Noah Foster was ever so slightly changed. "A guy," I said as I nodded. "Got it."

"It's just...that guy was...and you were..." He shrugged, licked his lips, and looked everywhere but at my face. "Obviously, you know how to catch a guy," he said in a hoarse whisper. "And I want to know how."

I opened my palm and thrust my arm forward. "Noah Foster, I'm going to make a fuckboy out of you. Just help me pass this one course."

The slightest roll of his eyes at the word I used to describe his future self wasn't missed, but he gave me his hand to shake. "Fine. I'll...find time. Tomorrow night."

"Tomorrow night it is," I said, shaking harder. And when I slapped his shoulder fondly, he nearly toppled into the bookcase, but he grunted and I released him.

I left him in the library with his phone number programmed into my phone, doing my best not to add a skip in my stride, and decided to burn this energy off at the gym. Avery and I were supposed to be conditioning already, but I'd gone on a very fruitful stalking mission instead.

I had thirty or so hours to figure out how to make the awkward, stammering, intimidating-as-hell Noah Foster into a desirable bachelor. It seemed like a task that would require months of careful consideration, except I didn't have that kind of time.

Then again, I was a great improviser.

I stopped by the team house to pick up my gym stuff, then joined Avery, who was already mid-workout by the time I changed and climbed onto the treadmill. For twenty minutes, I did cardio warm-ups and I considered Noah's predicament. First, I would need to get to know him a little better and see what his interests and qualities were. I was browsing for his unique selling points, so to speak. Mine were easy. I was a star goalie, swift and nimble. And if I had one quality aside from my on-ice talent, it was personal branding. I'd find Noah's image even if I had to carve it out for him.

Nerdy. Smart as hell. Cute, if not exactly dripping with sex appeal. But also intimidating with the size of his brain and the sharpness of his argumentative tongue.

"Whatcha smirking about?" Avery asked.

"Huh?" I brought down the speed on my treadmill and pulled out an earbud. "Was I smirking?"

"It's the Sawyer equivalent of being head over heels." He opened his water bottle and sucked several deep gulps down his throat, then wiped his brow with a towel. "What's up?"

"I think I solved it," I said. "My physics problem. The Noah problem."

"Oh yeah?" Avery lifted his thin eyebrows. The right one had two lines shaved off in the outer third, giving him a rebellious look. "How so?"

I kept my pace steady, breathing in and out evenly. This was the whole purpose of conditioning. I was putting all my fighter hormones to good use and training my body for speed and endurance. And I was mean good at it, too. Over my shoulder, I glanced at Avery. "I promised my soul to the devil."

"And here I thought you already promised your soul to the devil when he made you the fastest fuck on the ice I ever saw." Avery's sense of humor was on another level. His lips never quivered, but his sarcasm dripped.

"I did that, too," I said. Then I proceeded to tell Avery everything that had gone down between me and Noah while simultaneously cooling down and moving over to strength exercises. We were lifting dumbbells facing one another, practically competing which one could go further until our shirts were soaked in sweat and our faces red with heat. "And here I am," I finished. "Fuck if I know how to do it, but you can bet your ass I will."

"Tsk. I won't put my ass on the line," Avery said and it was encouragement enough. He thought I could do it. "Do a mock date."

"Maybe," I said, taking a minute to rest my numbing arms. "When he's ready. We'll try theory first. He wouldn't expect me to build a rocket before I learn Newton's laws, right? Same thing."

Long after the workout and the rest of the day consisting of matches of table soccer, I lay in my bed and stared at the ceiling. Avery was deep asleep, snoring every so often much to my chagrin. And I tossed and turned, unable to keep my heart still. I'd thought that scoring a tutoring session would be the solution I needed. But it was only the first step.

As for the rest. Well... There were a few more steps along the way. But it couldn't be that hard, right?

I had to actually learn all the shit Wallaby had failed to teach me for half a year.

I had to do it quickly, all the while outdoing myself on the ice in drills and in matches.

And, on top of it all, I needed to teach a nerd how to get laid as effortlessly as me.

Great. At least I put all these impossible challenges in a nice, bulleted list.

FOUR

Noah

I WAS MAKING A HORRIBLE MISTAKE.

I was wasting everyone's time and this was going to be a disaster.

When I saw Matt on Sunday afternoon, I told him as much. What I failed to mention was the intensity of the blush that remained on my face long after Sawyer Price had walked out of the library and left me wheezing in the scent of his cologne. I also didn't tell Matt how Sawyer's scent reminded me of spring in the mountains and nature welling with life, bursting with new energy, and the world turning green with hope.

"Um, I thought I was your wingman," Matt said.

"I hate to fire you, but I haven't exactly gotten much action," I said. "Besides, the guy's got experience with other guys. Maybe that's the difference."

Matt, over the top, rolled his eyes. "I've got experience with guys, too," he muttered.

"Practicing kissing me when we were thirteen doesn't count," I said. We'd both walked away disappointed from that one. I'd hoped to be into him when it had happened, but I most definitely hadn't been. And Matt had hoped the same, but soon realized that me being a boy was actually a deal-breaker. It had felt like kissing an inanimate object that you loved a lot. He was my best friend, but he was absolutely not someone I wanted to kiss.

He raised his hands in surrender. "Very well. I'll clear my desk."

I crumpled up a piece of paper I'd been reading old notes from and tossed it across my room at Matt, who was sprawling on my bed. "I was hoping you'd help me cancel Sawyer," I said after a moment of silence.

"Hmm." That was it. Matt narrowed his eyes in thought and tapped his lips with his index finger.

"What?" I asked. "It's obviously a silly idea. I don't know what got into me to say yes. He's really fucking good at convincing people to do shit for him."

"Language, young man," Matt said.

Neither of us laughed at that anymore. We'd had that joke going on for ages. My parents were very stern about the way I spoke and were the examples of politeness. I'd once said 'damn' in front of them and Matt had witnessed the reprimand. He hadn't let go of it since. And I never thought twice about the language I used so long as I was out of my mom's earshot. "Seriously, he's good. He wouldn't let me pass until I said yes. And then he kept badgering me with doing anything it takes in return. Fuck. How did I let this happen? I'm supposed to be smart."

"Not people smart," Matt said offhandedly. "But if he's so good, maybe you really should give that two-way tutoring thing a chance. We could all learn a lesson in getting what we want."

"He's gotten to you, too," I said in despair. When I

checked the time, I realized we were a mere hour away from the dreaded meeting. "Any chance you'd go to him and find an excuse for me? I'll let you bring your next three dates to my room."

Matt rubbed his chin in a grand display of mock temptation. He'd asked me once to do that and I had. My room was approximately three million times more impressive than any in this dormitory. The date had gone all wrong when the girl turned out to be a big sci-fi nerd like me and asked Matt all about the posters and stacks of novels, to which Matt probably just went cross-eyed because his interests were firmly set on everything but science fiction.

"I don't think so, buddy," Matt said. "You'll just have to face him and tell him that yourself. And because I know you can't possibly do that without falling through the ground, I'll rest assured knowing that you'll learn the lessons he teaches you. Then you'll teach me, too, and we'll rule the whole wide world." His hand moved through the air in his field of vision like he was showing me the wonderful future in which he had all the power of the entire planet. I shuddered at the thought of mandatory tacos for breakfast every Tuesday and beer pong replacing democratic elections.

I sighed. "Fine. It's too late to cancel, anyway. He'll be here in an hour."

"And you're supposed to teach him all of physics?" Matt asked with a doubtful tone.

"Sort of."

He nodded and pondered that. "An aggressive hockey goalie and a temperamental genius who's actually scared of strangers in the same room. I can't wait to see how this plays out." He laughed out loud as I pointed to the door.

"Get out."

He laughed harder and hopped up from my bed, then blew me a kiss and wished me luck. "Don't kill each other."

Matt left me to simmer in anxiety over letting that puck-chaser into my room and promising to teach him the most complicated and universe-explaining scientific field in existence. The thoughts of Sawyer in my room, at night, droning on about the ways to seduce a guy made me sweat as much as the idea of me lecturing him on the formation of galaxies and the phenomena that black holes were.

I checked the time and decided I could go out for a walk in the cold and crusty snow that covered the ground. February was just around the corner and this winter was only reaching its middle, but I was longing for spring. And not just because Sawyer's cologne had made me think of it for thirty hours straight.

I walked and walked all over campus until my cheeks were numb and my nose was frozen. When I returned, some fifteen minutes before the appointment with Sawyer, I undressed and hurried to shower off the sweat that had only just cooled on my body.

Just when I stepped out of the shower and tied a towel around my waist in order to moisturize my face, I discovered a new fact about my latest student.

Sawyer Price was not punctual.

Four minutes early, he banged on my door. I cursed under my breath and hurried to let him in before he knocked the door off the hinges. "I hear you. I hear you. Alright." I pulled the door open and his fist froze in the air while his eyebrows shot up and jaw fell down.

"Oh, wow, okay. Shit. Nice welcome." His dark

brown eyes dropped down the length of my bare torso to where the towel was well secured. "You're actually cut. I'll be damned."

"Come in," I said and moved to let him pass.

He swaggered inside like he owned the place. "Cool room, man. Are you gonna put something on or did I misunderstand the sort of practice you're asking for? It's not a definitive 'no,' if that's the case."

"Stop talking," I huffed. How was he even keeping his face straight when he said those things? And how was he not stammering and tripping over his words when he suggested that? I was already nearly trembling. "Gimme a sec." I hurried away, picking up some clean clothes and bumping into the door of the closet which unhooked the towel from the hip. It fell away with all the grace of a curtain call, but I managed to snatch it and spin around.

"Ass. I saw ass." Sawyer was dead serious when I spun to face him, clutching the towel over my crotch.

"Turn the fuck away, dammit," I snapped and walked back into the bathroom. There, I wanted to flush myself down the toilet and never appear anywhere where there were humans again But because I couldn't, I put my clothes on, splashed my face with cold water, replaced my glasses, and walked out with the reddest face I'd worn since the night Sawyer spilled vodka all over me in front of a hundred college students. "Can we just pretend that none of this ever happened?" I croaked.

Sawyer, comfortable in my spinning office chair, one leg hanging over the armrest, nodded. "It's actually good news. You've got a nice build."

His words strangled me. Discussing my build wasn't how I'd imagined this night unfolding.

"Half your problem is what you're wearing," he said.

"Consider this your first lesson. You want to attract attention without seeming like you want attention. Have you noticed how everyone looks like they just want you to leave them alone? And that makes you want them more? That's the trick. We need to go through your wardrobe and find what kind of clothes show off your body without seeming like you're showing off." He tilted his head. "Following?"

"Not a bit," I said, widening my eyes. He looked so comfortable in my chair and in my room. If our places were swapped, I would be, at best, sitting with my back straight at the edge of the bed. And even then, I would feel rude and like I was overstepping the boundaries. "I need to look unapproachable? But also desirable? That makes no sense. You said it yourself. I'm scary."

"Eh, there's scary and then there's *scary*. You, my friend, are intimidating because you're smarter than everyone else in the room. Like, when we spoke yesterday, I couldn't tell if you were mocking me." He swirled the chair left and right .

"I was," I admitted.

"Rude. Anyway, the other kind of scary is the sexy kind. You get me?" He looked so hopeful that this style of teaching would work.

"Nope. You lost me again," I said.

He exhaled, then straightened in the chair. Suddenly, all the relaxed, laid back layers of his image were peeling away. What remained was a sideways look at me, a little pout on his lips, narrowing eyes, flaring nostrils. Right. He looked sort of scary. Like he was so done with this shit. Like a cat that had just been offered lettuce for dinner. But he also became twice as hot if that was possible.

Shut up, my brain reminded me. Sawyer was here for a reason. He wasn't a canvas for my virgin ass fantasies.

But he looked like he could sweep me off my feet any moment now and I wasn't sure if I would find the strength to say no. My breaths grew shallower and I discovered that I was holding my lower lip between my teeth.

"See?" Sawyer asked, his voice a little lower and huskier.

Fuck. Me. I crossed my arms on my chest and thanked the Maker for baggy pants that concealed all the filthy, sinful things that were happening inside my banana-decorated boxer-briefs. "See what?" It was a strangled attempt at concealing how my body reacted to his aura.

He tilted his head and raised his chin, the smallest of smirks touching his lips. "You see," he concluded. "Now we just need to make sure you can pull it off."

"What? Like, now?" Panic crept into my voice. "I was gonna teach you a learning technique tonight."

"You will," he said as he got up and approached me. The scent of grass and leaves and a cool mountain breeze washed over me and I wanted to squirm and rub my thighs together. "Sit here," he said and pointed at the chair. "Let's see you relax."

"I am relaxed," I lied.

"Unless you lost a baseball bat up your butt, you're gonna have to try harder," Sawyer said. He fell onto my bed, legs spread casually. His black cargo pants were tucked inside his *Doc Martens* with red laces. His back rested against the wall and the Christmas lights gave him a halo. He didn't even blink at suggesting there was a baseball bat up my ass while I needed to claw at the armrests of my chair as the words rang through my skull. It was like he was intentionally embarrassing me. "Wiggle your shoulders."

I made circles with my shoulders and tried again, harder, when I saw visible dismay on his face.

"Better," Sawyer said. "Slouch a little, but, like, without slouching. You know?"

"I...really don't know," I said, leaning against one armrest, then the other, then leaning back and forth, looking for some position.

"When were you on your last date?" Sawyer asked, a little more somber.

"Um, a while ago," I lied.

"How did that happen?" he asked.

"Grindr." Another lie. But it was an easy one to swallow.

He cringed. "And how did that go?"

"Not...great." I didn't need to invent much. The fact I was incapable of speaking of these things was already plain. As was the apparent fact that my wardrobe was doing me more harm than good. "I'm not a people person," I said. It was true.

"Grindr isn't a people place," Sawyer said, waving his hand dismissively. "The rules are all different. People greet each other with dick pics. Not that I'm judging, but it sort of kills the fun for me. I like the chase, the flirting, the seduction. Jumping into someone's bed when you've already seen their dangly bits ruins the thrill. There's no mystery in it."

"Uh-huh." I agreed in theory. The one attempt at hookup apps had been enough to inform me I was not that kind of a guy. No shade on those guys, but I also wanted to catch someone's eyes from across the room, push and pull for a while, see if there's chemistry before taking it elsewhere.

"Have you ever picked someone up at a bar? Or let someone pick you up?" Sawyer was all matter-of-fact about it, like that was something ordinary. I guess it was for him.

"Um, no. Never. Like I said, I'm not…"

"Friendly? Forward? Extroverted? Got it. We'll make do with what we have." He stretched his lips into a smile.

I sucked my teeth and directed my gaze right at him. "You know what? You're kind of a dick."

He snapped his fingers and pointed at me, his smile morphing into a grin. "How do you do that?"

"Do what?"

"That. How do you grow a pair when you need to bite back?" He was way too amused by this.

"I swear to God, I'll send your ass out and eat ice cream on the day you drop out." I crossed my arms as I leaned back. We were on my turf, after all.

He just wagged his finger. "Maybe that's who you are," he said. The excitement that was rising on his face reminded me of Archimedes spilling the excess water from the bath and discovering how to test whether the king's gold was real or not. Except, Archimedes ran naked all across the city before the idea evaded him and there were no hints that Sawyer would be undressing any time soon. "Maybe we should build your brand around that. Because you are a coy fucker. Just don't take it so far because, like I said, it scares people off."

"So far, you've told me to be scary, but not too scary; welcoming but unapproachable; attractive but without trying. I'm genuinely not sure if you're teaching me or making fun of me." I didn't let my gaze waver before him.

He nodded like he understood. "I'm not making fun of you. These lessons are all I have to save my ass. I'll make you the most desirable guy on campus if that's what it takes to save my career. Now, focus. Narrow your eyes. Give me a pout. Never fix your glasses with the back of your hand or with one finger pushing the bridge. Instead, take the frame with two fingers and fix them like you mean it." As he spoke, he moved to the edge of the bed, pumping me up for my grand fixing of the glasses.

I furrowed the space between my eyebrows and did as I was told.

"Hawt," Sawyer said firmly. I couldn't tell if he was kidding. "You're not just a brainiac nerd next door. Hell no. You're a lean, mean, fuck-machine. Say it."

"I would literally rather jump out of the window than utter those words," I said.

"Fine. But keep saying it internally. And believe it. You've got a little beard shadow on your chin and a hint of a mustache. Your hair is messy." He was scanning my entire body.

"I mean, I'll fix it. I just showered." I hadn't realized I would need to be in my best shape for the first lesson.

"What? Oh no, these are the positives. Keep it like that. It's stylish, but casual. Like you don't care that you didn't shave or that your hair's perfect the moment you wake up. Wear it like it's precisely what you wanted and the pillow made it because you're a dude who gets what he wants." He was nodding harder as he spoke, getting more into it with every word. "Let's see your wardrobe. Go and put your best outfit on."

I exhaled with dread, then dragged my ass to the closet and began rummaging through my clothes. My dark blue pants were the best fit I had according to Matt, but they stuck to my legs and packed everything way too tightly. I preferred the comfort of sweats or baggy jeans.

I moved my hand through my shirts and found a light green one. Matt had called it "*muy caliente*" when we were at the mall and I got it on a whim. I felt tight in it, but Matt said it showed off my body.

"You talk an awful lot about Matt. Are we trying to impress him?" Sawyer asked.

Only then did I realize I was saying all of this aloud. "I, um, no. No way. We're just friends."

"You ramble when you're nervous," Sawyer diagnosed me. "Gotta keep a check on that mouth."

I snorted, then marched into the bathroom. He'd already seen me in a towel and went way overboard with his comments. I wasn't going to undress in front of him. Besides, I couldn't trust my body not to betray me. My dick had already been hard once in the time Sawyer had been in my room and I was losing my patience.

When I walked out, I reached for a bowtie and suspenders to complete my look. My shirt was already buttoned up all the way, but Sawyer leaped across the room and shut the closet, nearly chopping my hand off. "Oh, no. Got a belt?" he asked.

I did.

"Brown. Good. Brown is good," he was saying as I pulled the belt through and buckled it up. It was a thin one, not drawing too much attention to it. It wasn't too bad, but I preferred the suspenders if I had to choose. "And no bowties until I can trust you to wear them like they're a crown. We're going for simple, elegant, contemporary. Leave Bill Nye the Science Guy behind."

I met his gaze as we faced one another and shot him a glare of my own. The corners of his full lips were quivering as he squinted and scanned me. His hands reached to my neck and I held my breath. We were a foot apart and his fingers touched the top button of my shirt. He popped it like he'd done that a million times.

I swallowed way too loudly, making his exhale a soft laugh. "Another, I think." And before I could disagree, he popped another button and tugged my shirt apart. "Much better, but you could do with a smaller size to really make your torso draw the eye."

"While simultaneously acting like I don't want any attention," I said.

"Exactly. See? You're catching on quickly." As he spoke, I looked away. His gaze was excruciatingly thorough all the way down to my red-and-black-striped socks. "The moment the snow melts, you're changing into ankle-height socks and rolling up your pants. Show some skin down there. Show the Victorians."

"Hmpf." I shifted away from him. His body was a furnace. His scent tickled my nostrils. His proximity turned my guts to steel. I was going to get hard again and I needed to abort the mission. "Right. How about we discuss physics?"

It felt like the tension between us disappeared at once. Sawyer stepped back, seeming a little smaller. "Right."

"I thought I could show you Richard Feynman's technique to learn anything." Even as I spoke, his attention drifted to the rest of my room. He approached the posters and examined the planets on them.

"Uranus?" he asked, pointing at an orange and brown one.

"Um, no," I said. I had no idea why he'd think that. "It's just an imaginary gas giant."

He nodded thoughtfully. "Uranus is a gas giant."

"No, it isn't." The moment I answered, I replayed his words in my head. "You are a child."

He threw his head over his shoulder to face me and shared the most blissful smile you ever did see. "Hit me. Feynman something." He plopped his ass back into my desk chair and I decided to take the spare, wooden chair from the corner, then sit next to him. Normally, it was the other way around, but I had a sense that everything would be a battle with Sawyer, so I preserved my energy.

"Richard Feynman was a physicist in the quantum and particle field. He won a Nobel prize for the diagram he had made that depicted particle processes."

"Careful, there. You're losing me." Sawyer said that with such casual disregard for everything I held dear that it warranted an eye-roll.

"Anyway, he is also famous for the particular way he learned pretty much anything he wanted. Take the material you want to learn. Say, this chapter in your textbook." I lifted the textbook for Physics 101 and opened one of the early chapters.

"Where'd you get that?" Sawyer asked.

"The library. After you ran away." I put my finger at the top of the chapter and traced all the way through the first page, then flipped it to the second and third. It was explaining the most basic laws of nature. "Read through it. Twice if you have to."

"Oh, buddy, I read it ten times already," Sawyer said. "All of it."

"Good. Then, you should be able to take a piece of paper and explain it as if you're teaching a sixth grader," I said. "And as you try to do that, identify the things you don't know or understand. Then, go back to the material and read those specific parts. Take a book on them and find explanations. Look for references in the back which might point you to the right book. And when you fill one knowledge gap, identify another. Do this over and over until you understand the whole chapter and are able to teach a child. Rinse and repeat."

He watched me and hesitated. "Is…that it?"

I shrugged. "That's how you'll do it with me." I was soft spoken on that part and looked at him until something clicked in his eyes.

"Alrighty. Where do we start?" he asked.

"Right here. The basic forces that govern our world. Gravity, which governs the attraction between masses and keeps planets in orbit as well as you in that chair. It keeps the universe together. Electromagnetism, which is basically the interaction between electrically charged particles. And weak and strong nuclear forces. The weak one is part of radioactive decay and it won't be on the test. The strong one, basically, keeps all of the matter stable because it binds protons and neutrons together." I frowned at him because his eyes were glazed while I was talking about the entire universe in the simplest terms I could find.

"Not to brag, but I've heard of gravity," Sawyer said.

"That would be sarcasm," I decided.

"Correct." He sighed. "You're losing me with all the electrically charged particle nonsense."

I scratched my head and tried harder. "Imagine balls."

"Now we're talking." His evil smirk was horrible.

"I've changed my mind. You're not a child. You're a teenage boy. Particles aren't really balls, but we draw them that way because it helps us imagine them. It's ironic in a way. We are made of this. We are particles that got together and decided to figure out what particles are." I waited for a chuckle.

I received an ogle and a quiver of his eyebrows. "Your sense of irony is precious."

"Right. Balls. Imagine them. They are charged with electricity. Okay? Okay. And electricity makes them attract or repel one another, depending on how these balls are charged. Positive or negative. If they are the same, they repel each other. If they are opposites, they attract each other."

"That sounds about right. Put that lesson down into your book, too," Sawyer said with a coy smile.

I was well aware that I was attracted to my opposites. I had always been the best of friends with other clever cogs. But I had always had a thing for mean athletes who thought running the fastest was going to change the world somehow. "That's basically what electric force does. And the magnetic force is the product of the motion of these charged particles. A fridge magnet and your fridge are charged differently and they slam together."

Sawyer leaned back in my chair and watched me, his butt practically hanging off the edge and his legs spread in a way that gave me unholy ideas. He tilted his head. "Got it."

"Good. Now, let's try to understand all of the universe and a single atom at once," I said, rubbing my hands.

Sawyer pretended to faint and slid off the chair until gravity won once again and his ass slammed against the carpet.

It dragged a near smile from me, but I managed to wipe it away before he opened his eyes. I observed him coldly and waited for him to get serious and back in my chair before we proceeded. For an hour, I was lost in my world and I talked without a break while Sawyer asked questions and told me to slow down and, most often, found a way to make physics all about smashing butts together.

I wasn't going to show that I appreciated the creative way of looking at things.

But by the end of the first session, I wasn't as reluctant to schedule the second one.

FIVE

Sawyer

HOLY FUCK, MY TUTOR WAS SECRETLY A HOTTIE.

This thought followed me the entire day on Monday, all the way through lectures and practice in the evening. On the ice, I was an unstoppable force of nature. There was a single puck I let slide in the instant my attention wavered and I thought of Noah's towel incident.

Not smart. I needed to drop him from my mind much like he'd dropped the towel off his peachy ass. Not that I was thinking about it that much. It just popped into my head. And it popped into my head again and again.

And when that puck went right by my stick, I wanted to curse myself and Noah together. I rolled my eyes and played on, slamming my stick against the ice only once.

After practice, I took a hurried shower and raced back to the house to go over my notes the way that guy Feynman would have done. The buzz of hormones that were still coursing through my veins after the battle on the ice made me squirm and lose my attention quicker than I liked. I drummed my desk trying to go over my source materials to better understand the forces that kept an atom whole.

In the textbook Noah forced me to take, just a page after the dry and boring explanations that wouldn't sink into my memory, there was a note.

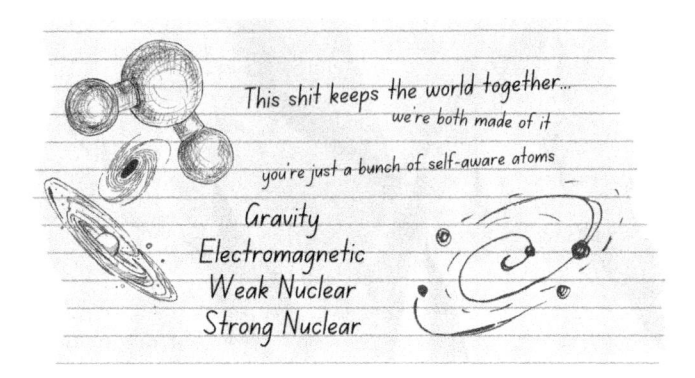

> *This shit keeps the world together...*
> *we're both made of it*
> *you're just a bunch of self-aware atoms*
>
> Gravity
> Electromagnetic
> Weak Nuclear
> Strong Nuclear

I lifted and examined it, then realized my facial muscles were stretching my lips wide and I shook my head. "Such a nerd."

Avery barged in and I tucked the note back inside the textbook like it was porn, then shot him a look over my shoulder. "What's up?"

He tossed his duffel at the bottom of the bed and nodded at me. "Great work today."

"Yeah, you too," I said.

He circled around the room, went to the closet, then began changing into his nicer clothes.

"Leaving?" I asked.

"Yep. Got a date. Sort of." He was walking in and out of the bathroom for the next few minutes, each time looking more like the fuckboy he was.

I understood the urge better than most people.

Hockey was a mean and physical sport. When the game was over, your body was still in battle mode. Testosterone ran high long after you took your skates off. And, frankly, sex was never better than after a long, hard game.

I envied Avery for having a date lined up. He got to vent these needs just fine. And me? I had a tutor I wanted to impress tomorrow after practice, so I needed to put the work in.

I spun in my chair, watching Avery do final checks before leaving. "Think of me," I singsonged.

"I will *definitely* not be thinking of you," Avery said and winked, then went out.

I was tempted to go down and play a round of table soccer with Tyler or Sebastian. Or to go to the gym and run until my energy was spent. The bloodlust and, well, lust in general burned in my chest as I pressed my thighs together and gripped the edge of my desk, staring at my notebook.

Lines of text I had written there were blurring before my eyes and from the mist a shaggy, honey-brown head of hair was slowly emerging. The pissed-off expression and the secretly amused green-eyed look behind those black-framed glasses remained before my eyes even when I closed them and leaned back in my chair.

Fun was a strong word to use. But the guy had made physics bearable. And, all in all, I was glad I had an appointment tomorrow night. Which was really fucking weird considering that his job was to talk nonsense at me and we had nothing in common outside our mutual tutoring agreement. I'd invited him to the game I would play against the *Breakers* next week, but he had looked at me like I was speaking in tongues. And he'd told me about a book that had nothing to do with my tests just because he thought four hundred pages about the entire life of a star would be a fun way to relax. So yeah, I definitely didn't know which part tugged on the corners of my lips when I thought of tomorrow's session, but one of these forces from the note was pulling me to his room.

I CLIMBED THE STAIRS OF THE BIG DORMITORY and marched down the hallway to Noah's room after Tuesday's practice. As I neared it, I checked the time. Seven minutes early. I'd always figured it was better to be early than late, but after the towel incident, I wasn't so sure.

The thing was, as I neared his door, I couldn't get it out of my head. Two days had passed since his perky, round butt had made itself comfortable inside of my mind. And his cut torso. And the blotches of red heat on his cheeks after he dressed. And the way he held his breath when I unbuttoned his shirt to make him look more casual. What would have happened if I'd tried to show him a quarter-tuck? Poor guy would have fainted.

Or I was just imagining things.

I paced the hallway for a hot minute, then knocked on the door anyway. If he was naked, so be it. I would live with the memory. And if he wasn't, better yet, because I wouldn't have to think of what these things meant.

Noah's footsteps were soft on the other side as he approached and opened the door. "Early as ever."

"Fully dressed," I said in a way of greeting.

He snorted and shut the door after me. "I anticipated your lack of punctuality, so I adjusted."

"You don't have to adjust for me. I'm not butt-shy." I dropped my duffel, cursing myself internally for talking about his butt to his face. He was immediately scratching his head and looking around like there was a way to escape my comment and I was, yet again, butt-dreaming. Dammit.

Playing it cool, I plopped into his chair just to annoy him and examined his attire while he moved to the bed and sat on the edge. He had prepared himself for scrutiny, that was evident. The pastel green flower-pattern on his white shirt went well with the color of his eyes and hair. The black pants, not so much, but you couldn't argue with a classic. Truly, his appearance was not what was stopping him from storming all the bars. "Do you have more clothes like that?" I asked. "That shirt is like a really fancy candy wrapper."

"Is...is that...good or bad?" He stiffened all over.

"It's delicious is what I'm trying to say." I tilted my head and looked at him from another angle.

"Oh." His ears perked a little. "It's...the only one I have."

"We should go to the mall one day. You want more shirts like that." I put a pin in that, then leaned back and slid down his chair. The incredulous look that briefly crossed his face was probably a comment on the way I sat, but I didn't care. I was comfortable. "What kind of music do you listen to?" I asked.

It looked like he was thinking about this a lot already because he took a deep breath and opened his palms in the air in front of him, really trying to grab my attention. "Okay, so, there's this guy doing various punk arrangements of those epic classical pieces. Like Vivaldi's *Winter* but cyberpunk. Or Tchaikovsky in dieselpunk. It's really cool. You should tota..."

"Nope." I waved my hand to stop him right there. "I trust it's fun, but you look like a Tom Odell fan. If you tell people anything else, they won't understand who you are."

Noah licked his lips, annoyance flaring on his face. "Hold on." He hopped up and crossed the room, reached to the top of the shelf for a wireless speaker, then pulled his phone out of his pocket. Now that he was standing still, I got a good look at his pants. We could improve the color, but this was definitely his fit. His butt was adorably packed and his waist was narrow, but his legs weren't too thin and...holy-fucking-shit this guy was not a Ken doll. His crotch, when he turned all engrossed in his playlist, came into full view and I wheezed, swallowed, and nearly choked on saliva.

"You good?" Noah asked without looking at me. He moved on before I survived the shock of seeing his sizable bulge. "Here it is." He tapped his screen and set the speaker on the desk, then returned to the bed. When he sat down, he leaned forward, slouching, making himself appear both lanky and smaller.

I listened because it was a great excuse to be quiet and let my body cool down. The fact I had come here straight from practice, my blood still boiling and the hormones still swirling, wasn't helping.

The tune of a harpsichord and various wooden percussion were joined by strings and finally an accordion. Even though these aesthetics had nothing to do with any of my interests, I wasn't immune to the vivid images of airships over smog-clouded cities, cog-based gadgets, clockworks, steam-powered robots, and gaslit streets. Steampunk to the music of...

"Beethoven," Noah said, as if he read my mind. "His Seventh Symphony."

I rolled my eyes. "Fine. That's pretty cool. But don't tell that to people. Not everyone's as open minded as this guy." I said as I shot my thumbs back in my own direction. "I'm a hard rock and metal fan, but if I played my favorites your eyelashes would melt."

"I could have guessed that," Noah said and gave me a casual scan.

"Rude." I pursed my lips for a moment. "But true." I wore mostly black and my body was a canvas for line-art tats. I was aggressive on the ice and a handful off of it. Deducing my music tastes didn't take a lot of brain power even if Noah had so much to spare.

He sniffed and smiled. "So, what else?"

"Hmm. If you start talking about astrology, you might as well go home. Unless you're meeting a chaotic twink who starts that conversation first." I thought about it a little more. "Actually, the less you talk, the more mysterious you seem. Let him ask the questions and keep your answers short. Act like you have no interests whatsoever. It'll look like your interests are too interesting. You know?"

"Got it." His song ended and another started, but this one was a lot heavier on synths and electronic music.

"What's that?" I asked.

"Atompunk. It's criminally under-appreciated. It's got all the analog beauty and all the futuristic optimism." Noah was obviously into it. I looked over my shoulder to where his posters were. They seemed retro futuristic, too.

What the hell was I doing? He was passionate about

these weird and wild things and I was teaching him how to hide that. I inhaled and held that breath for a few moments, then looked into his eyes. "What's your goal here?"

"Wh-what do you mean?" he asked. He had a way of parting his lips in surprise just after he'd licked them, so the lower one glistened with wetness. And those breathtaking green eyes watched me intently.

I exhaled. "I'm not gonna pretend I know anything about dating," I admitted. "I'm a fisherman, if anything. I know how to reel them in, but I don't know how to keep them."

"So?" He cocked his head a little like a confused puppy.

"So, if that's what you're looking for, then maybe I'm not holding up my end of the bargain very well. I can't give you tips on how to make someone fall in love with you." That was a trick I had never learned.

"Fall in love?" Noah's voice turned squeaky. "I don't...erm..." He cleared his throat and lowered the volume on the speaker at a really epic bit of his atompunk thingy. "How about I master tossing the hook into the pond, first, before we worry about, um...this metaphor got away from me."

"Choking on the bone?" I suggested and cackled to myself while Noah's cheeks turned red and lips pressed tight. He rolled his eyes at my dirty sense of humor.

A moment later, he lowered the volume some more, then gestured with his head at my duffel. "Got your notebook?"

"You bet," I said. "I found your note yesterday."

"Did it help you memorize the forces?" he asked.

"Which forces?" I played dumb. "I liked the doodles."

While he snorted and shook his head dismissively, I grabbed my duffel and tossed it into my lap, then unzipped it to find the textbook, pen, and notebook for the lessons. I left a clean uniform in my locker and filled the duffel with my sweaty one. I had been stupid enough to pile up the garments over the textbook, so I had to rummage through them now.

The stink of sweat wasn't too terrible, but the real kicker was the moment when something hard dropped onto the floor under the desk and we both looked. Not that I was easily embarrassed, but Noah was for both of us. His face burst into flames when his gaze landed on my well-worn jockstrap with a hard, plastic cup.

"Um...you dropped..." He pointed at it and looked away, biting his lip.

I chuckled to brush it off, but the temperature of the room was abruptly increasing. Dropping jockstraps, no matter how unsexy they were in their purpose, around hot nerds at the height of after-practice horniness was a sure way to make stupid decisions. And the stupidest decisions were always signed by Sawyer Price. I grabbed my jockstrap and laughed harder. "This old thing?" I held one elastic strap and swung the whole piece of gear around. "It saved my junk more times than you could imagine. Nothing can get through this. Check it out." And for some blindingly stupid reason, I tossed my worn jockstrap right at my physics tutor's horrified face.

He caught the plastic part with both hands. "Ohmyfuck." His eyebrows curved hard into a huge frown as he tossed the jockstrap right back at me.

Whatever Golden Retriever existed somewhere in my genealogy, his instincts kicked in and I caught the strap, then tossed it back, my monkey brain assuming this was just a game of softball.

"Fuck." Noah grabbed the jockstrap, then dropped it into his lap, then lifted it, then dropped it again. I laughed for the lack of anything else to say and watched as he carefully picked it up and frowned while examining it. "You wear this?" he asked, his voice jumping up by an octave.

"Yep. Keeps me from losing my best qualities." I shrugged guilelessly and bit my lip. Somewhere in the back of my mind, a tiny voice of reason was squealing in excruciating shame. This was definitely one way of dealing with a potentially awkward situation. Dial it the fuck up.

"But you wear it over something, right?" The look he gave me was almost pleading.

I bit my lip apologetically. "Er, it depends. Some guys do. Paxton, Riley, Sebastian. They wear compression shorts under the strap. Me? I don't bother with shorts at all. I like to be nimble."

"Oh god," he whimpered and handed the jockstrap back to me.

I released him from the torment and took the plastic cup in my hand then stuffed it back inside my duffel. For the lack of any words that would make this easier, I laughed. And to my surprise, Noah laughed too. Strangled and high-pitched, yes, but it was laughter nonetheless.

He grew smaller when he pressed his thighs together and slouched a little more. "So, um, jockstraps aside, do you have your books?"

"Oh, right. Yes." I dug through my duffel and found what we needed. Dog-eared and ever so slightly carrying my after-practice scents, the stuff was in a pretty good condition, I thought.

"Okay. Let's dive in." And, as he moved to the wooden chair next to the soft desk chair I had occupied, I found myself checking him out. Noah, however much that kept surprising me, was seriously a piece of eye candy. My gaze followed his tucked shirt and found the irresistible bulge that made my mouth water. Except, as my heart sped, I noticed his bulge had grown bigger.

Right. Maybe don't throw your dirty jockstrap at a guy you're coaching on how to score a guy, I told myself as I found some energy to look away. Oh, but it was hard. Both the object of my desire and the act of looking aside. It was hard as fuck.

For the next hour, we had our heads together, and Noah doodled on a piece of paper while explaining how dimensions worked. Something about adding time into a bowl of soup and different planes of reality. He soon became so engrossed in the likelihood of us living in a simulation and I had no idea how we'd gotten here. I figured I must have been thinking about something else in the meantime, but I had no memory of what. Instead, I was staring at the expressive way his lips moved and the confident, heated tone of his voice. "So when you think about it, it's almost certain that a technologically advanced civilization would run a simulation. Need I tell you about *The Sims*? And if we can agree on that, then we agree on the fact that the simulated reality will also evolve enough to run a simulation of its own. In theory, this spirals into millions of levels of simulation. You stack them one on top of the other, deeper and deeper and deeper. But there's still only a single reality, the one that started it all. So, when you think about it, the odds that you and I exist in that single, real reality, could be one in a million. Or one in a billion. Or however many levels of simulation you can imagine. And that's the problem with theory, Sawyer." He looked into my eyes with blazing passion. "When there's something you can't prove or disprove, you better stay away from it. It's sort of like God. Are you religious?"

I blinked, way too absorbed in the mossy greenness of his eyes to follow his tangent. "I mean, I have sex with guys as often as I do with girls and it's all pre-marital, so go figure."

He snorted. "Right. It would be like a deer worshiping the Church of the Crocodile."

I liked the way he said it. It made me laugh.

Noah, too, laughed, albeit softly. "I could give you a million arguments that we're trapped in a simulation, even though it won't change the fact you need to pass your physics test anyway. And you can never disprove it. Whatever you say, I'll have an explanation. That's the trouble with the ineffable concepts that explain themselves. It's better not to go down that rabbit hole."

"Hm, good that we dodged that one," I said reassuringly.

He picked up on my sarcasm. Progress. "Right, well, I'm just making a larger point that physics explains everything around us. If you know how to listen, you'll realize that it rhymes."

Our heads were so close to one another, like two conspirators plotting. He looked at me and I waited. There were stars in his eyes, glimmering, bursting with energy. This guy was in love with science. He was so deeply into it that no guy ever stood a chance. I was doing this whole thing wrong. I was teaching him how to attract a guy. But what I should have been doing was holding mass lectures on how to get Noah Foster to like you. He was so much more than what he presented. All these guys I was about to unleash Noah on had no idea what was coming. They weren't ready. There was no way they could ever make him happy. Hell, I doubted they'd be able to satisfy him.

I licked my lips as my stomach hollowed and tingling filled it. Nervousness I couldn't explain itched at my fingertips.

He sigh-laughed and pulled away from me, looking at the notebook in front of us.

Though I didn't have many coherent thoughts in my head and I hardly knew what I wanted to do or if I wanted to do anything at all, the moment Noah pulled away, my chest was filled with frustration and sadness. I felt like I'd just missed an opportunity to…do something. My ears rang and my face heated up.

Noah turned the session around and focused on the test materials from my textbook. We had two weeks to cover these or I was doomed. I didn't regret the time we lost in the heat of his lecture. It was the most fun I had learning anything.

We lived in a simulation, apparently. Even though nothing changed, it made me look at the world a little differently. Maybe it gave me a small amount of extra courage. Or a flicker of hope. Maybe something unattainable and unlikely could happen thanks to a glitch in the system. Maybe that was what we called miracles. Maybe there was a chance for me to… What? Pass physics, of course. But it suddenly seemed a little less important. I just didn't know what I was comparing it to.

When I left Noah's room later that night, the wild

post-game hormones had faded away, and walking on the slippery path between his dormitory and my house felt more like walking on a really thick featherbed. My heart thumped faster and I felt like some progress was made. Bit by bit, meeting him three times a week, I would make it. I was sure of that.

The other thing I knew for certain was that I really looked forward to Thursday night. I'd visit Noah after practice, intruding on his private time, but I had a hard time feeling sorry. Listening to him was the closest thing to the thrill of skating that I'd ever felt. That had to mean it was worth it.

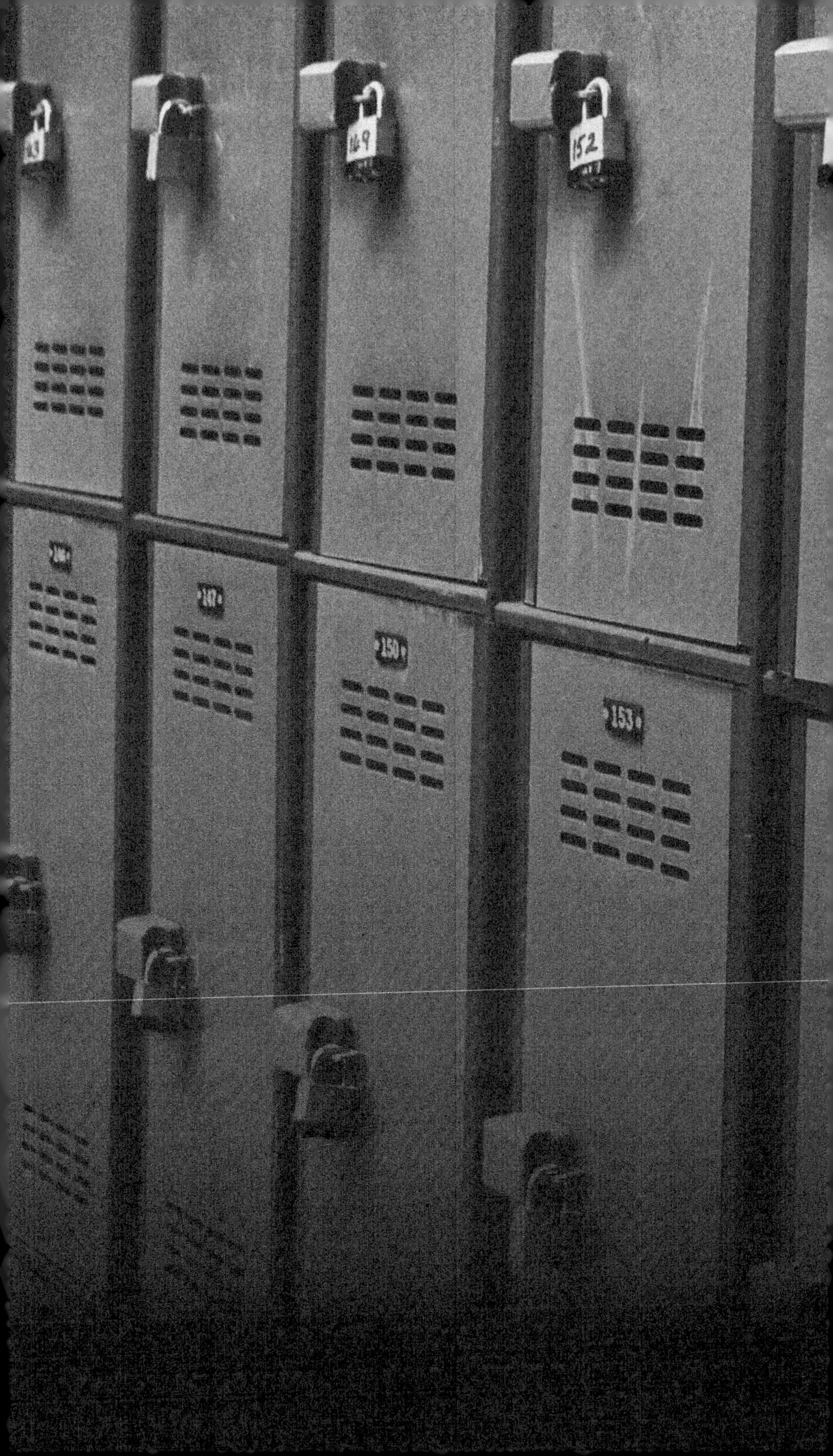
149
152
150
153

SIX

Noah
___

ON SATURDAY, JUST A LITTLE AFTER MIDDAY, I saw one of my regular students out of my room, and startled when someone loudly banged on my door right after. I'd been expecting him, but not yet. It spared me the pacing when I opened the door and found the ever-sullen Sawyer Price leaning against the door frame. "Ready?" he asked.

"Not even a little," I huffed, rolled my eyes, and walked out. "Let's go."

He swaggered shoulder to shoulder with me, the contrasts almost ridiculous. My walk was steady, back straight, head held high. His was that of a cartoon character with way too much confidence. "Busy morning?" he asked.

"You can say that again." A yawn stretched my mouth open and I hurried to cover it. I'd had tutoring sessions since seven with only a breakfast break in between. Had Sawyer not insisted, I would have continued as planned. I would have had a lunch break on my own, then more students, until Sawyer came by in the evening for his session.

Over the last two weeks, I had grown fond of those sessions because they were the last in my day. In my head, Sawyer was equal to resting, even if we still did all the learning and the awkward conversations about my dating tactics, of which I had none.

Sawyer, for his part, was getting the hang of the basics fairly quickly. Whether it was the notes I kept leaving in his textbook or Feynman's technique or the fact that we droned on and on about the same concepts session after session, it hardly mattered. He understood all he needed for the first round of tests next week.

I glanced at him from out of the corner of my eye. He was normally slightly taller, but the way his torso leaned back when he walked evened out our heights. His eyes were always a little narrow as he observed the world around him with a heavy dose of skepticism, as if it might not be real. Perhaps it was because I'd convinced him we lived in a simulation, although that hadn't been my exact goal with that topic.

He wore a bomber jacket over a black hoodie and black cargo pants that seemed baggy but actually fit him to perfection. His entire wardrobe was like that, as far as I could tell. Dark, seemingly ill-fitting, but all his pants hugged his ass for the best possible outcome. It was always big and firm. I figured that being an athlete had something to do with it. My own gym membership off campus was barely worth the money I was paying with how often I showed up. And even that was thanks to Matt, who practically dragged my ass there with him. "Nobody knows you there. Nobody's gonna look at you. It's good for your health. It'll make you look hotter." And so he went on and on and on until my will broke and I joined him.

Sawyer had his duffel hanging on the small of his back, the long strap crossing his torso from the right shoulder to the left hip. "You had practice?" I asked.

"All morning," he said in his broody, husky tone.

Two out of the three times a week, he came to our sessions straight from practice. The first time, he'd flung his jockstrap at me which both horrified me out of my mind and turned me on to a painful level. Since then, he was sharing his jockstrap less and minding to pack the textbook on top of his clothes more.

Over the course of the past two weeks, I noticed a little difference in him. Whenever he came to me straight from the rink, there was something like wildfire in his eyes. There was elation in the way he walked and spoke and there was heat coming off his body long after he should have cooled down. The third time, when hours had passed between a game and tutoring, he was a lot more subdued. Maybe even a little awkward.

I wasn't sure which I preferred. The slight awkwardness about his behavior matched my permanent state of being. The fiery interest in everything I said when he was fresh off the ice, however, put me into the center of his world for that one hour in the evening. Just the way he looked at me after practice felt like he was seeing the most interesting spectacle in the world.

Now, he glanced at me, his cheeks rosy from the cold, and the same sparks glimmered in his eyes. "We're playing against the *Breakers* next week. You should come and watch."

"I don't think that's your best idea," I said, running out of excuses.

"But you should," he insisted. "Have you ever seen a hockey game?"

"No." The word dropped from my lips incredulously. When would I have seen one? I mean, sure, there was a rink on campus, but that was like asking the devil if he'd ever gone to a Sunday mass.

"Then you have no idea if you'd like it or not," he said.

I snorted. "Guess how many times I was told that about trying to date a girl." I didn't need to have dated a guy or slept with a guy to know they were my only interest. I knew Sawyer was bi because I'd seen him unashamedly being torn apart by those twins. He couldn't exactly relate to this feeling, and good for him. But I knew where my interests were.

He cringed, his brow splitting with a frown. "I don't care for bigots. But this is different."

He had a point, except I really didn't care for hockey. "Do you want me to watch the game or you?" I asked bluntly.

He chuckled at that. "You got me. I'm not a sexy winger, so I get fewer eyes and have to source all who might agree to watch me play."

"I knew it." After a moment, smiles spread across both our faces, and the oddest fuzziness filled my chest. I was silent, trying to push those weird feelings aside, as we left campus behind and sought the metro line to the outskirts of town and the mall Sawyer had insisted on.

When we boarded the train, it was blissfully void of the crowds. Unlike his hockey game, I was dreadfully sure. I sat by the window and Sawyer sat across the aisle from me. An odd sensation that it was a missed opportunity filled me out of nowhere. It took active mental gymnastics to come to the realization that I had been expecting a fuller train. In such a case, Sawyer might have had to sit next to me. And in such cases, our legs might touch in passing. And in such cases...

I stopped myself right there.

Just because he was tutoring me on how to appear more attractive, there was nothing to indicate he would see me that way. After all, we never met on Friday nights. He liked to have those for himself, if I remembered correctly.

And that's perfectly fine and normal and I have no problem with it. It was a practiced line I repeated to myself whenever I caught myself thinking about Sawyer keeping his Friday evenings to himself. Or sharing them with whoever he wished.

He was just here to teach me things. And when he praised my figure or my pose or something I said, it meant nothing. He was merely encouraging me so that I could score a guy when we took this to some bar.

Sawyer was restless on the train. He took his jacket off and fanned his face, then ran a hand through his hair. I liked the way it arched over his brow and closed around his face. Every facet of his entire appearance was meticulously curated, I was certain. He wore his expressions and his look like he wore his boots and his nose piercing.

He hopped up and grabbed the railing high above his head with both hands, crossing his legs at his ankles, and lifted himself in a chin-up.

I observed him, thrown back into my younger years when boys around me did acts like this for nothing else than that they were bored. Sawyer's hoodie lifted as he lowered himself and an inch of bare skin on his steely abdomen flashed me and squeezed air out of my lungs.

How exactly the motion of an object that was Sawyer's body affected the crushing forces on my chest was a mystery to me. There was more at play here than merely physics.

I looked without looking, equally enthralled in this boyish act as I was annoyed that a grown man could not sit still. I was as attracted to those moments when his skin bared as I was appalled at his lack of care for public property and his image in the micro-society that those few people on the train constituted.

And yet, I watched him, biting my lip against smiling, and pretending that there weren't flutters descending from my stomach right into my groin. Every bit of me tingled with acute interest.

Then I remembered to breathe, too.

Sawyer dropped from the railing and onto his feet, then dusted his hands against one another. "That feels better."

"Better how? You just wasted energy." This was the best I could do to cover up the fact that I had grown thirsty while looking at his body and that pointless display of his strength.

"I'm sore all over," he said as he dropped into the seat next to me.

"And this helped?" There was genuine, scientific curiosity in my voice.

Sawyer nodded. "It stretched my muscles and warmed me up."

"Well..." I looked around. "I'll only ever know that in theory."

He cocked his head to look at me. "Don't fuck with me. I saw you shirtless. You can do a chin-up."

"Tsk. I can barely do a pushup." I shrugged. The mere

reminder that he'd seen me in nothing but a towel, which dropped moments later, was enough to heat up my cheeks.

"Bullshit. Try one." He was dead serious.

And so was I. "No fucking way."

"Try a chin-up, Noah," he insisted.

"I'm not making a fool out of myself in public," I whispered.

"Just in private?" he teased.

I pursed my lips and flattened my eyebrows over my eyes.

He was relentless. His fingers dug into my ribcage, piercing me through my jacket.

I squealed and yelped.

"See? You've made a fool out of yourself already. A chin-up won't kill you." He was grinning like an ass.

I looked around, embarrassment threatening to set me on fire. Not a single person looked my way. A guy was dozing over two seats on the far end. A woman was reading a book with a shamelessly sexy cover model that made me slow down in my gaze over the train. Nobody cared.

"Chin-up! Chin-up! Chin-up!" Sawyer clapped his hands at each syllable and I stood abruptly to shut him up, if nothing else.

I grabbed the railing along the ceiling and tightly gripped it, mimicking what I'd seen Sawyer do. I crossed my ankles while still standing, then lifted my legs off the floor only to hang like an orangutan. My lanky, long arms couldn't pull me up if my life depended on it.

Then, what little dignity had been left to me, disappeared. Sawyer placed his hands on the outer sides of my legs, his fingers reaching as far as just below my butt. And if the way he eased me up so effortlessly wasn't humbling enough, the proximity of Sawyer's face to my crotch definitely was. Has anyone ever told him not to put his face so near a virgin's dick and balls? He didn't know I was a virgin, though. But if he remained so close and caused my body to react the only way it could, he might start to suspect.

I did a hasty chin-up, mostly pushed by Sawyer and his hands sliding higher up my legs, then dropped down and fell across from him, leaning in as my cock stirred and thickened.

My breaths were shallow. "There," I huffed. "I can't do a chin-up."

"What are you talking about? You did a whole damn chin-up just now." The grin on his face was bordering on evil. I would have called him out on it if he wasn't so damn adorable.

The rest of the trip was thankfully somber. We filed out of the train and back to the city surface, then Sawyer practically dragged me to jaywalk across the street. The mall was one of the more contemporary ones. There was something oddly elegant about it. It was different from the usual food court, cinema, and arcade malls of my high school days.

We walked in and Sawyer became the alpha dog of our pack to the last atom of his being. He led the way up the escalator and all around, while I was desperately trying to catch up with his determined stride.

And when we walked into the first store he chose, he simply marched on. He moved through the aisles and scanned the clothes before I could let any of it sink in. He was throwing shirts at me without asking me for my preferences. It was oddly liberating.

Aisle by aisle, he piled me up with shirts, sweaters, T-shirts, and pants. "Don't worry. You'll buy what you want. But you'll try on everything."

And so the longest hour of my life began. Sawyer, who was a hockey player and a wearer of near-exclusively black clothes, fancied himself a fashionista. And, as he gazed between me and the pants section, I wondered what else his talents were.

"We're good for the first round," he announced. And here I was, thinking he'd given me enough clothes to try on for the rest of the year.

If there was a way to speed up the process through a quirky, nineties montage and be done with this personal hell of mine, I would have done it in an instant. I wouldn't even ask what it cost. But I actually had to undress in the changing booth approximately forty-two thousand times.

On his insistence, I tried a pair of faded red pants that tucked my butt tightly in the stretchy denim. And as I was picking a neutral colored T-shirt, to pull over my bare torso, the curtain of my booth flew aside and Sawyer rocked his head. He examined me shamelessly, though he was only interested in the fitting of my pants.

"Do you think you can go a size smaller?" he asked. "I'm dying to see it."

"I, erm, don't think..."

"Wait there," he said and disappeared.

I sighed and began taking the pants off. Just as I was free of them, the curtain flew back again and I wanted to scream.

Sawyer was holding the same red pants, but smaller, and grinning as his gaze dropped to my black boxer-briefs.

"A fellow cucumber fan, I see," he said huskily and I

looked down to the green cucumbers printed all over my underwear.

I snorted, rolled my eyes, and yanked the pants from his hands. He was so casual with near-nudity and indecency that it was both infuriating and deeply erotic. And I couldn't decide which pushed my buttons harder. Either way, putting the pants on now that my cock had stirred again was a huge challenge. Not that I was bragging. And not that I had much to compare myself to other than the surreal standards of size in porn. Still, I struggled to zip myself up over the growing bulge.

Why the fuck am I getting hard? Panic flooded me. He'd merely seen me in my underwear and I was already falling apart. I stood absolutely no chance with a guy who had any intention with me whatsoever. If we ever found a guy like that at all.

Desperation and anxiety mixed in me as I held a T-shirt in my hands and practically froze in that position. Even when Sawyer pulled the curtain aside again, my reaction was slow. It was so slow that he scanned my bare torso, the ill-fitting pants, and the bulge that might or might not have been an obvious erection.

My hands and the T-shirt dropped to my crotch to conceal myself, which was the telltale gesture that made Sawyer's mouth work silently for a moment and eyes peel wide open. "Um...too tight," he said, voice strangled. "And red isn't your color. But it was worth a shot."

I nodded. I could have told him as much before all this torment.

He still stood on the other side of the booth, curtain pulled and held by his arm. We stared at one another for an endlessly awkward moment. Sawyer breathed in, his chest rising, his eyes darting all over me.

"Um." It was all I was capable of saying.

He knew, without a shred of doubt, what was going on in here. And down there.

I winced. "Curtain?"

"Right," he said and nodded jerkily, still looking at me with pinking cheeks and glazed eyes. He had this look late at night when we studied together, too, if practice had preceded the sessions.

The realization struck me out of nowhere. He was horny. A little, but enough to show. The way his ears perked and his eyes narrowed and his teeth sank into his lower lip should have been enough to tell me as much. Then again, I'd only ever seen such looks on TV. People didn't exactly exhibit lust in my general direction.

I wheezed in and licked my lips, somehow bringing Sawyer back to his senses. It was like he had been looking at someone else for a moment. It was like he slowly saw me the way I was, and not some Adonis that he had imagined in his lust-filled brain. He frowned and nodded, then dropped the curtain as he stepped back.

When I changed back into my own clothes and stepped out, my problem had deflated enough that I could rest assured it wasn't drawing any unwanted attention. And when I met Sawyer, he was his normal self, too. He smiled and showed me a huge pile of clothes. "These are the pieces you're allowed to wear. Greens and blues are your best colors and all of these emphasize your figure. You just have to choose the ones you like."

I blinked at him, then at the pile. He had picked up every last bit of clothing that had felt vaguely comfortable while I had been trying it on. All the ones I liked even a little were on one pile. And all the ones that had made me feel too lanky or skinny or cramped in their tightness were gone.

Sawyer tapped my shoulder and said he'd go and look around if they had anything to his liking. I stayed with the pile of clothes and wondered how many pieces were too many. I had a healthy balance from basically tutoring during all my waking hours. I had a scholarship that paid me a small allowance on top of my accommodation and tuition fees. And my parents were generous enough with their money, if not with their emotions.

As I sifted through the dark blues and deep forest greens, then all the brown and gold and silver accents that Sawyer had picked up for me, I couldn't choose. At random, I picked up a little over half the things Sawyer had approved and carried them to the register.

Out there, while my stuff was being scanned, I watched Sawyer. He had his bitchface on. The unapproachable and desirable kind. He had mastered the contemporary mating calls, evidently, but as I looked around, there was nobody I could imagine Sawyer eyeing. He just wore that expression when he wasn't deeply immersed in something.

And when all my stuff was packed, Sawyer needed to help me carry it back to my room. Our conversation was sparse on the way back, mainly because I was equally tired and embarrassed of the near-horrible encounter in the changing booth. It was bad enough as it was. It could have been even more devastating, had he pulled the curtain back ten seconds sooner.

But when we marched into my room and dropped all the stuff on the floor, Sawyer sat down on my bed rather than finding an excuse to go back to his. "I was thinking, after my test, we could put together a little test for you, too."

"Oh, yeah?" I asked, starting to unpack and fill my closet.

"We'll do one of the bars in the student center," he said confidently. "It's a controlled environment and the guys there are the easiest because they're looking for the same thing. We'll go in separately, but I'll be near you to observe. And if it goes wrong, I'll just sweep in to the rescue."

I grinned at that. "How wrong could it go that I would need rescuing?"

Sawyer laughed. "If you look like you're on the verge of combusting, I'll know."

I joined him in laughing at the worst case scenario knowing well enough how likely that was. If someone even tried flirting with me, I would explode with embarrassment. And equally so if everyone just pretended I was a ghost and turned away from me.

Anxiety soon pressed down on my chest and made breathing in a little harder. "Let's focus on your test, first, shall we?"

Sawyer nodded to that and the look of determination eased me a bit. "Play us some of your weird cyberpunk, will you?" he said.

And though I had expected him to leave any minute, the fact that he showed no intention at all pleased me. I hurried to hook up the speaker to my phone and find a good playlist while Sawyer kicked back on my bed, hands under his head, and a blissfully tranquil expression on his face.

My heart tripped and I wasn't sure if it was the nerves over the impending test date or something else entirely.

SEVEN

Sawyer

To say anxiety was debilitating before my first physics test would be putting it mildly. Last night, I'd done pretty poorly in drills, but last week's game against the *Breakers* had gone in our favor, so the performances evened out in Coach Murray's eyes.

The team supported me. This morning, as I marched out of the team house, they all cheered for me. And it was a boost I hadn't realized I needed.

The day brought warmer winds that melted the crusty snows almost into extinction. And when I realized that I could see the blue sky rather than the gray overcast clouds that had remained in place since November, I was genuinely inspired to remain on campus and on the team.

I had studied hard and I had paid my dues. I could do this goddamn test. I could do it.

Except, as I walked into the faculty building and into the mass of worried students who anticipated this same test, all my confidence faded away.

I talked to no one else and my mind started drifting away from the task at hand. I needed to think of physics and the tutor who had put so much effort into getting me ready. Or not. Why would I think of my tutor? He wasn't supposed to be a factor in this. He was hired to do a job, right? It was the same to him either way. But, as I found a chair and unzipped my backpack to check my notes one last time before we were allowed into the lecture hall, I recognized how badly I wanted to make him proud.

But why exactly he would be proud of a near-failure like me was a mystery I didn't want to worry about just now. Instead, I flipped through my notebook quickly and startled when a note fluttered out of it and into the floor.

I was grinning before I even picked it up. The fucker had done it again.

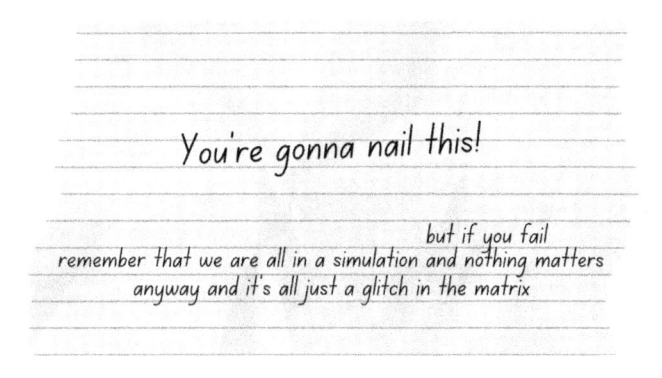

> You're gonna nail this!
>
> but if you fail remember that we are all in a simulation and nothing matters anyway and it's all just a glitch in the matrix

I read the note twice and barked out a laugh that rang against the walls of the hallway. "Fuck you," I muttered and folded the note carefully, then tucked it into my pocket for safe keeping. I'd collected several notes from him and they were all in the same style. An uplifting little message with existential dread tacked onto it.

My heart did a little dance solo in my chest and fear returned as Professor Wallaby stormed the hallway and let us all into the lecture hall. There, we were given an open question test and ninety minutes to fill it out. So, when I was finished in fifty-five minutes, dread filled me to the brim.

These things were calculated, right? She wouldn't have given us an hour and a half if an hour was enough.

I went through my test, twice, just to make sure. The basic theory I had answered well enough. There was one question that required solving a mathematical problem, which I had skipped entirely. But there was no way it would require anyone half an hour to solve if solving was an option.

The truth was, I didn't know if I'd answered anything else correctly at all. Every concept Noah had tried teaching me had faded from my memory. The questions were convoluted at best and blatant traps at worst. So, I sweated and shivered and tormented my lip with all the might in my teeth until I realized I would die if I had to sit in here another minute.

I tore myself off my seat and carried the filled out paper to Wallaby's desk like I was carrying my own execution warrant. I set it there, suffered her cold gaze of dismay, and turned away to practically run from the lecture hall.

Outside, I finally exhaled, and I took a deeper breath of air that moved the cogs in my brain. I had obviously made a horrible blunder.

I gritted my teeth and marched straight to my room, then dragged Avery to the gym. Quiet as ever, Avery simply looked at me for a moment, then nodded his full understanding. For nearly two hours, all we did was quietly work out. From the treadmill that burned my energy down, to the full body exercises, free weights, and some calisthenics that I could endure, this preoccupation with pain and exhaustion was all that kept my mind intact.

It was in the locker room, after we had showered, that Avery finally asked the question. "That bad?"

"Probably worse," I said, my muscles searing, knees trembling.

He nodded and spared me pitiful looks. Words were unnecessary here. We knew it was only the first of many tests this semester, but it was a blow to my determination should I fail already.

And if all else failed, at least I could find some comfort in living in a simulated reality, like Noah said. Mine would be a boring gameplay, some cottagecore where I did a lot of woodworking and bird feeding, and very little ice hockey.

I dreaded meeting with Noah again. I didn't know how to tell him that all the hours he had spent on me had been a waste.

As days passed, my temper grew more subdued. What was left in me was a sense of shame that, despite all the efforts, I had done so blatantly poor that I couldn't even identify my own mistakes. Down the drain it all went. Feynman's learning technique and Noah's approving nods. So, when a week passed with no updates from Wallaby on the student portal, I decided I owed Noah at least the truth and the repayment for his efforts. We still had one test to get through. The test of his skill at the bar. And I hoped to God he would do better than I had. Otherwise, I had no reason to waste more of his time.

I visited him after Wednesday's practice to make plans for Friday night. After knocking on his door, I waited for the soft footsteps and the turning of the doorknob. On the other side, rumpled-haired and a little flushed, Noah stood shirtless and barefoot, wearing only a pair of shorts.

"Er, do you ever wear anything when you're alone?" I teased, my mood spiking instantly. The warmth and the appealing subdued yellow light of his room pulled at my heartstrings.

Noah was ever so slightly surprised to see me, but he stepped aside to make room for me to come inside. I hesitated, but stepped in anyway. "Heating's been broken since this morning. I can't breathe in here."

As the door shut, the heat of his room dazed me. "Then open a window," I pointed out.

"Seems wasteful." That was his reply as he made his way to the bed and sprawled on his back.

I laughed and sat in his office chair, my duffel dropped by his desk. The heat was enough to make me just a little uncomfortable in my jacket and hoodie and the tight T-shirt I wore underneath, so I peeled layers off.

Noah gulped and watched me from his bed as I pulled the hoodie over my head. In the process, it had lifted my T-shirt all the way to my armpits. Once I threw the hoodie onto Noah's bed I fixed the T-shirt, but he had already taken a long look at my body and his face was even more heated. It was no wonder he needed coaching in these things. Even with me, the type of guy he'd never consider twice, he seemed short of breath and on the verge of stammering. And I'd only flashed a little bit of my skin in the most innocent way possible.

I wondered, when we went out on Friday, and when Noah came across some hot and smart jackpot guy like himself, what he would be like. When he was talking to someone he was truly attracted to, would he be a disintegrating mess?

I'd be there to lend a helping hand, of course.

"I haven't heard from you," he said and I realized we had been silent for a long time.

"I...didn't wanna bother you," I said.

The smallest frown ever wrinkled the place between his eyebrows. "What about the test?"

I shrugged. "No results yet," I said simply. I didn't have the heart to tell him I'd wasted his time. He could have trained a smarter guy on building spaceships by now. But a dummy like me couldn't handle the basics. It was like my mind was prickly but all of physics was smooth and I stood no chance of ever fitting that knowledge somewhere in my head. Deciding to steer clear of that topic, I smirked. "What are we gonna do about *your* test, though?"

"My test?" His voice went squeaky.

"Are you free on Friday night?" I asked.

He snorted. "I don't have a date if that's what you mean."

"I was more worried you had a brainiac coming over for hard drills in quantum mechanics." I winked at him and he licked his lips, then pursed them.

"I'm trying to hear an innuendo in what you said, but it might be too advanced for me," he admitted.

I laughed out loud. Odd. I hadn't laughed since I'd read his last note. "I think you're ready to try hitting on someone," I said. "Pick your own outfit from the approved selection and we'll go to the *Thirsty Thinker*. The atmosphere there is more welcoming than at the *Brewhouse*." I suggested the tavern because guys at the *Brewhouse* knew how to cut deep with their eye-rolls. I'd been on the receiving end of a few in my heyday. Tougher crowd, but they knew how to show you a good time. Still, it was a little more advanced and I wanted to test Noah in a simple first date interaction. "We'll scan the place, find a nice guy for you, and try a few icebreakers. No pressure."

"When people say 'no pressure,' it only adds pressure," Noah muttered. "I don't think I'm ready."

"Of course you are," I insisted. "All you have to do is not fall apart and run away. Try a pick up line. Hit me."

"Um, are you a Wi-Fi signal? Because I'm feeling a connection." He cringed.

I cringed harder. "Whoa, that's bad. We'll stay clear of pick up lines. Keep in mind all I've taught you. Pout, glance, glance again. Hold eye contact, then look away. Meet eyes one more time, do a little 'Sup?' and wait to see what the climate is like. If he's cold, look around so he sees you don't really care. That'll get him thinking."

Noah growled. "Fine. But when I send all the wrong signals and the guy thinks I'm threatening him and there's a bloodbath, it'll be on you."

"I'll take those chances," I said.

We caught each other's gazes and held them a moment, then Noah looked away. Just like I'd taught him. The yellow glow of the Christmas lights above his bed and another from the lamp on his nightstand faded the shadows on his body. The dark green shorts he wore were high on his nearly smooth legs and the waistband was low. While he had decent abs, the V line of a shredded body wasn't present, and it made him look so much more natural. He was lean and smooth and somehow vulnerable. His lithe body seemed breakable if only someone mishandled it. And his heart... I didn't even know what to think of it. I could only vow to make sure whoever we targeted on Friday was decent. Fuckboys were off limits, that much was for sure. Our nature was to have fun and think of consequences later. But Noah didn't deserve that. His expressions were too soft and his eyes too full of wonder and fear.

My heart clenched when I realized I couldn't look away.

Friday came sooner than I anticipated, but Wallaby still hadn't graded the test. I was slowly but surely getting ready for a failing grade. Even accepting it. Though sixty points was all I needed, I was prepared for half as many. Frankly, her lateness was the most infuriating, if the least surprising. Some odd night, she'd ping us all with our results, and it would come from out of left field.

Noah waited for me in front of the dormitory, his eyes narrowing in a sneer of superiority. "I beat you at your own game."

"Or I brought you down to my level of tardiness," I said casually, shrugging to really drive the point of carelessness home.

He looked horrified for a moment, then hesitated, and finally started walking. "I wish I was doing anything else in the world."

I laughed. "I felt the same way during my test."

Tonight was later than our usual meeting times. I'd returned from a game this afternoon, licking my wounds with everyone else on the team after we lost despite our best efforts. Exhausted and defeated, we had all retreated to our own ways of coping. Riley sulked, Cameron played his nerdy games, Tyler and Sebastian got far more competitive in table soccer, Beckett was off to hook up no doubt, Avery was a blank canvas, Caden disappeared. Paxton and a few others went out to some party. And me? I was about to test this awkward genius in the dating games.

"Come along." I gestured with my head and we started walking. The student center was in the heart of Northwood's campus, surrounded by recreational facilities, then faculties, and finally, the larger areas reserved for accommodations and sports as well as a few labs which couldn't fit into the faculty buildings. The center was noisy almost all the time. During the day, all the seats were occupied by coffee-downing students. During the night, those same students poured copious amounts of beer down their throats.

And considering we were about to enter a tavern, I had a beverage in mind.

The *Thirsty Thinker* was as busy as ever. Two girls and a guy worked the bar that was almost completely dotted with guests. The taps were running endlessly as folks crowded around for their turn.

"Oh god," Noah whimpered.

"They're all a little drunk already," I reassured him. It didn't seem to mean the same thing to him as it did to me. He seemed horrified and I laughed. "That's a good thing. Clouded judgment is your friend."

"Gee, thanks." The level of sarcasm in his tone made me proud. The boy was learning.

I found us two spots at the bar where a brunette girl sat on the right side and a couple of empty stools extended to the left. My plan was to give Noah a boost of courage, then leave him on his own while I struck up a conversation with a girl. That way, any onlookers who might scan Noah would know for certain that I wasn't someone to be worried about.

As we neared the spots, the brunette looked up and caught my gaze, gave a jerky nod of greeting and didn't wait for me to return it. Mentally, I rubbed my greedy hands and checked her out a little more thoroughly. She was sculpted to perfection, each curve exactly to my liking, and the highlights in her hair gave her a polished look that begged for a bad boy to taint with his proximity and influence. But I turned away from her, both to seem uninterested and to focus on the test at hand. "Could I have a red ale?" I asked the bartender when he reached us.

"I'll have what he's having," Noah said, his voice insecure.

"You will not," I said, incredulous. "He'll have an American pale ale, a lighter one." The waiter glanced at Noah, then nodded to confirm my order.

"What was that?" Noah asked.

"I'll let you have a sip when they arrive. You'll thank me later." We perched ourselves on the worn, high bar stools and brought our heads together as if we were conspiring. "Do you see anyone you like?"

"Erm…I wasn't looking." He frowned.

A scoff escaped me before I could stop it. "Looking's kinda important."

"Right, but I still think this is a bad idea," he said, then bit his lip. "I thought I was ready, but I'm really not."

"It's not a big deal, Noah. Just talk to any guy. Even if you don't like him. Try out the eye contact I taught you. You were doing so well in your room." I wanted to grab him and shake some courage into him.

"Yeah, but that was in my room." He seemed even

more nervous now. "Was your first time like this? I bet you were all cool about it."

I inhaled a shallow breath of air, but it cut off when the meaning of his question failed to fit inside my head. "First time?"

Noah blinked, as if he was surprised by my question. "What?"

"What 'what?'" I leaned in closer. "What do you mean, 'first time?'"

The bartender set our beers in front of us. I barely heard him over the rising concern.

Noah was reddening at an alarming pace. "I mean, you know? A date. Picking up a date. I…"

I leaned in even closer, practically brushing our noses against one another. "Noah, is this your *first time*?" I emphasized the term so there was no mistaking my meaning.

Noah bit his lip and looked at me guiltily.

"Fuck," I hissed. "I thought you had Grindr hookups. Noah, you should have told me."

His eyebrows contorted in even more guilt. "I lied. Fuck, I'm sorry, Sawyer. I panicked and said it because it's frankly embarrassing. See? You're already looking at me differently. And it sucks. Yes, I'm a virgin. And you know what? It's time to grow a pair and be done with it. I'm sick of people treating me like a child. I'm not a child."

I watched him, baffled, as his thoughts raced and he rambled. "Are you sure? Maybe this isn't the best idea."

Noah closed his eyes and took a deep breath. "I'm sure," he said, opening his eyes and straightening. "I just want to be rid of it. It's not that big of a deal, right?"

I had a hard time making myself lecture him on how the first time should be special. My first time was anything but that. And the following two were awkward affairs with other girls. I'd never had a sweetheart who I wanted to share that special moment with. And I'd never found one, either. Still, I said, "It's not my business to tell you, but if you pull the plug now, I won't consider the test failed."

Noah snorted, then took my beer. "A sip?" And, at my gesture, he tried the red ale, then screwed his face into a sour expression. "Fuck. That bites." He tried his own, then, and his expression relaxed a little. When he was less thirsty, he nodded to me. "Stay there if I make a fool out of myself, but let me do this. If there's any luck in this simulation, we're in the last hours of my virginity."

I shook my head. Part of me thought he was rushing into it. Then again, he was twenty-one. I'd lost my virginity at sixteen, then hooked up with my first guy when I was eighteen. I had plenty of experience and a lot to regret despite all my parents' efforts to teach me to make smart choices and give me the safety to make mistakes.

I wanted Noah to do this the right way, but I was the least qualified person on the planet to teach him that. If there was a right way to do it, I didn't know what it was. "But give it another thought, will you?" I urged him.

"I'm sick of carrying that baggage around," Noah admitted. "Even when people don't know, it's almost like they can tell. Like they can see I'm somehow…lesser." He grabbed his glass and took a deep gulp of his beer, then another. Courage filled him as much as the ale. He set his half-empty glass on the bar, then nodded at me bravely. "I'm done being lesser. Now, watch my back." He spun away from me on the bar stool and began scanning the crowd.

Deciding to keep my ears pitched to his voice, I turned away so I wouldn't hinder his chances. Nobody wanted to approach a guy who had an annoyed bulldog watching his back. And my annoyance was rising quicker than my mind could understand and keep up.

Something about this felt wrong on a level I hadn't considered before.

Noah was far too sweet and tender to go into his first time blindly.

"Can I help you?" The brunette was looking at me and I realized I'd been glowering in her general direction.

I softened my edges a little. "Dunno. Can you?"

She scoffed, then returned her attention to her phone, shaking her head while a sneaky smirk touched her lips. "You're all the same."

"That's a big statement," I said, but the touch of entertainment helped me get Noah off my mind. He was choosing this. A hookup to get it over with. He was ripping it off quickly after worrying about it for way too long. Not that twenty-one was late. We couldn't all be early bloomers like me. Besides, I knew plenty of downsides to that, too.

It seemed I wasn't getting Noah off my mind.

"Care to explain?" I asked, leaning a little closer to the girl.

"I've been sitting here for less than an hour. Can you guess how many players went through, trying to pick someone up?" She barely moved her gaze from her screen. A slender hand gently swept a lock of hair from her face before she lifted her green gaze at me. What I saw was Noah's gaze before I remembered he was behind me, looking in the other direction. But the striking resemblance in color and intensity made me wonder if he had a sister he'd never mentioned. I was sure he'd told me about being an only child. Still, it took a moment to put Noah's eyes out of my mind.

"I dunno," I told her. "How many?"

"Too many to count," she said with little interest in pursuing the topic.

"So it was a trick question," I concluded. "Aside from generalizing, what do you do?"

She chuckled softly, then shook her head. "I study anthropology."

"Ah, so generalizing should be a cardinal sin in your book," I accused. "And here you are, sinning like there's no tomorrow."

"Hi," Noah said behind me while the girl pursed her lips to suppress a smile and measured me.

"Hey yourself," a deep voice replied.

Noah audibly cleared his throat and I could sense his lack of breath. "Hi," he said again.

The deep-voiced guy laughed and Noah let out a nervous chuckle.

Bullshit, I thought. *There's no way he's that breathtaking.*

"So?" the girl asked me and I realized she'd spoken before but I hadn't been paying attention.

"Sorry?" I prodded. "I was miles away."

"I asked what a pious guy like you was doing wearing a goth body in a tavern," she repeated and I laughed out loud.

"I'm just a wingman here," I said, thrusting a thumb over my shoulder at Noah but not looking back. "As for the body I'm wearing..." I glanced down at my arms and torso. "Do you like it?"

"Smooth," she said, deadpan, then cracked a smile.

"Oh, um, physics. Erm. Sorry, yes. I study physics." Noah's smile was audible. "Oh, this? I think it's a pale ale."

"An American pale ale," I muttered into my red. It had a very pronounced alcoholic flavor and scent, though it wasn't the strongest red ale I'd ever had. It did bite on its way down, however. I exhaled.

Thankfully, the girl was picking up her phone again, drifting away from me just as we got going. It freed me to stew in my annoyance and the dirty little act of eavesdropping.

The macho voice asked something I couldn't hear over the goddamn crowd around us and Noah let out a squeal, then laughed. "I'm game," he replied. And when glasses clinked, I was certain they were theirs. "And what do you do?"

Too eager and interested, I criticized internally.

"I'm here on a football scholarship," the guy said.

Fucking hell. I rolled my eyes and busied myself with my red ale. Did he really want to go for an athlete? And a football jock at that? That was a big bite for anyone, especially if it was their first time.

I had expected Noah to go for a hot geek. Someone who would match his genius and challenge him. Not a dull football chaser. If he wanted a slow-but-sexy athlete, there were plenty more attainable ones to choose from. And with better reputations than the football fuckboys.

He could have picked a nice swimmer.

Or a bat swinger.

Or a hockey player? Preferably a goalie? Whose thought was that? Definitely not mine, I was sure. It made no sense. I mean, I didn't even like the guy. Sure, he was cute. And hot. And beautiful when he wore his baggy hoodie that hid his body like a gem you needed to work for. And he was funny and smart and kind. Something about him made me want to wrap him in bubble wrap and hold him until it was safe to come out.

Which was never. Football jocks would pry and lurk. They'd want to take advantage of Noah because he's so sweet and smart in all the academic ways, but not at all in the ways of guarding his heart.

"They don't really come around," Noah said and I realized I hadn't been paying enough attention. The girl was pretending I didn't exist and the jock was chuckling in that deep, attractive voice that made me want to mock his bass. "They sort of made me into who I am," Noah was explaining. The biggest perk of a tavern like this was that music wasn't dominating the space. Chatter filled the warm air inside and The Eagles' *Hotel California* played softly in the background, but I could hear Noah fairly clear.

He was sharing his life story with this stranger who didn't know him. It was very sweet of Noah, but it was a crucial mistake. He would either open his vulnerabilities to a random stranger or get mocked. Sharing stories of family was something I did with few of my dates and none of my hookups. It took safety and trust to open up like that. And I feared Noah was opening up to someone who couldn't appreciate it.

"I won this thing, this Physics Olympiad, when I was fourteen. It's not a big deal unless you are really into it, then it's pretty much like — what d'you call it? — that thing you watch every year that has all the expensive and funny ads."

"The Super Bowl?" The jock asked, chuckling.

Noah snapped his fingers. "Yes. That. I won the

Super Bowl of physics and, um, that became the base minimum they expect from me. I never won another one. And frankly, I didn't need to, if we're honest. I got my scholarship and all the connections I would ever need if I just keep studying hard. But it's never enough."

My heart cracked.

It was hard for me to imagine something like that. My parents were, if anything, too mindful of my needs. They'd spent all these years fussing over me, blowing wind into my wings no matter what I wanted to achieve. And whenever I failed, they were there to encourage me to get back up to my feet. They didn't have much to give in a way many students on this campus could flaunt, but they had given me more than enough. They'd given me a soft landing, no matter how tall my fall was.

It could hurt, for sure. Sometimes, it felt like seeing their disappointment would be easier than suffering through their spinning of all the ways my failure was "for the better, actually." But when I heard Noah, I realized how lucky I was.

Why hadn't he told me that? We'd spent countless hours in his room and he'd never mentioned his parents. Was he blowing this date on purpose? Or was the beer I'd ordered for him too strong?

I snuck a glance at his empty glass and my heart sank. Just then, the dusty blond jock threw his hand onto Noah's shoulder and gave an infuriating little rub. "That sucks."

Noah shrugged, oblivious to the true meaning of the touch, apparently. "You get used to it. I'm glad I'm independent."

And you will remain independent if it's the last thing I

do, I thought, then realized I was about to make him independent of a possible date.

"I wish I could do something to cheer you up," the jock said. By now, I'd turned all the way to face Noah's back and the interested jock's front. His hand on Noah's shoulder made me boil with anger. *You don't know how to treat him well*, I snarled internally. *You'll never know how to make him feel good. And you'll never know how to cheer him up.*

I tapped the jock's hand and gave him my most plastic smile. "'Scuse me. Pardon me. I need a minute with my friend."

"And you are?" the jock asked, but Noah was already turning around, blinking wildly and gazing at me like he was trying to communicate with me wordlessly. Alas, I didn't understand what he was saying with his eyes.

I ignored the jock altogether and focused on Noah. "We gotta abort."

"Wh-what? I mean, yes. Okay." He got up, then glanced at the jock with a confused look on his cute face like the spell had been broken. "Sorry. My friend needs me."

"Yeah, maybe I'll see you around or..." But neither of us heard the rest of what the jock was saying as we filed out of the tavern. The cold air bit my nostrils as soon as we stepped outside, the chatter dying behind the closed doors, but I didn't stop there.

I kept walking and Noah was catching up with my furious stride. Oh, but I was furious. I was mad at the whole world for some goddamn reason. Whatever it was, it drove me crazy; all my worst impulses were taking hold of me. I wanted to get into a brawl for no other reason than to lash out.

That fucker was such a familiar kind of player that it was disgusting. I knew every trick he'd pulled. He ran into a vulnerable, adorable guy, let him talk, showed fake interest, then made physical contact while hinting at all the crazy, sexy things he could do to make the cute guy feel better. Ugh. Every fuckboy in town had done that trick at least once.

It was cheap.

And Noah didn't deserve cheap tricks.

He deserved someone who would invent a new way of flirting for him. He deserved someone who wouldn't resort to tricks.

"What the hell happened?" Noah huffed as he followed me, almost shoulder to shoulder. "What did I do wrong?"

I stopped dead in my tracks. We had already left the bustle of the student center well behind and were following a path to his dormitory, rather than my team house. I hadn't planned it, but we were making our way to his place by instinct.

I looked into his big eyes where confusion was gathering. "What?" It was a gasp, rather than a question. "You didn't do anything wrong," I said.

A worried look bunched on his face instead of disappearing. "But I...I thought it was gonna happen."

"Not with him," I said, nearly growling, then took a breath to sort my thoughts. "I couldn't let you do it. I'm sorry." I stepped back. "It's not my call and I was rash, but I just couldn't sit there and watch you make that mistake."

"What mistake?" he asked, curious more than confused, now. He wasn't angry with me. Not exactly.

"That fuckboy," I said and the edged feeling I had

been holding so tightly leaped and showed itself fully. Jealousy. It fanned the embers in me into a roaring fire. "He was gonna take advantage of you, I could feel it. I know those guys. I know how they think."

"I'm not stupid, you know," he said flatly.

That stopped the words that had welled in my mouth.

"I know what he wants," Noah said. "And I told you what I wanted."

"I know, I know," I blurted, frown contorting the upper half of my face. "But there's so many other guys, less sleazy ones, who deserve you more. You don't have to just pick up the first one who's willing."

He was surprised now, his eyes widening and mouth opening. "Did you just call me a slut?"

"What? No. Hell no. I said there were better guys for you out there," I insisted. *Like me*, I nearly shouted, then knew instantly how wrong that idea was. I was no different than any other fuckboy around. In fact, knowing this probably made me worse.

"Where?" He demanded. There was a trace of accusation in his voice now. "If you failed to notice, nobody's ever interested in me."

"Bullshit," I spat. I didn't know why he was fighting me. I was only watching his back. "Plenty of guys are interested, you just don't see it because you're so certain that they wouldn't want you. Or you don't want them. Whatever the case, you've got better options than that hookup artist."

Noah pouted at me and I realized I'd totally wrecked his night out. "Don't you realize that I'm a socially awkward nerd who can't even talk to attractive guys?"

"Wrong. You talk to this attractive guy all the time," I

said, pointing at myself, then cursing myself for choosing that path.

"That's…different. You're not…I mean…" He huffed. "You're hot, but you don't look at me like that."

"Like what?" I asked.

"Like you're interested. And that's fine. I'm used to guys seeing me as their younger brother all the time and never as someone they would sleep with. But you wouldn't know what that's like. Everyone wants to get a piece of you." He said all of this like it was my fault people wanted to have sex with me.

But there was one thing he was totally wrong about. "I'm plenty interested, Noah. Don't think that I'm not. Fuck. You're smart *and* beautiful. What else could you want?"

He gaped, but I didn't let him speak even if he meant to.

"But I'm also trying to be your friend and do the right thing. Unlike Bluto over there." As the words spilled from my mouth, I replayed them and realized just how much I'd said aloud.

Noah stared at me like I was an apparition. He blinked, his green eyes glimmering under the street lamp. His chest rose and fell steadily. I hadn't realized how close we were standing to one another until he inhaled through his nose and nearly touched me with his chest. "You like me?"

"I…it's…" I pursed my lips. Fuck!

"Or you're just saying it to make me feel better," he concluded with his eyes narrowing.

"That's not at all what I'm doing. I like you. Okay? I like you a lot, but I'm also a player just like that guy was and that's not who you deserve." Darkness creeped into my voice as I said these things.

It felt like I'd eaten a rock. My stomach was heavy and my limbs were just kind of hanging from my torso, useless. My cock was stirring, for sure, and it only added to my annoyance. Of all the parts of my body, my cock had the worst timing.

Somehow, the thing that I considered a noble sacrifice of my own desires for the sake of a better outcome for him, annoyed Noah the most. His frown exploded on his face. "Can you stop doing that?"

"What? What am I doing?" I demanded, a tremor of hopelessness touched my voice.

"Treating me like a child," he said. "Can't I make a single mistake in my life? Does every first choice I make have to be the right one?"

I wasn't sure who he was speaking to. I hadn't realized I had been pushing him into doing anything like that. All I knew was that I couldn't watch him leave the bar with that creep.

"What I would really like, for once in my life, is to decide for myself what's right for me. Just once, I'd like to make a mistake." He said those things softly and I didn't know what to say to that.

I looked at him. He looked at me. And time ground to a halt.

The glimmer of the overhead street lamp reflected from those mossy eyes and the redness in his cheeks was only worse with the cool, late February air.

He gazed at me expectantly and I realized that all of me was tense. Every muscle in my face, my limbs, and my torso was taut. And, as I relaxed, I found myself nodding. "You should do that," I said softly. It was as good as promising to break his heart for the sake of gaining experience, but I did like this messy-haired, stammering, brilliant guy.

I liked him way more than I dared to admit to him or myself. And I definitely liked him more than some beefy brawler with no finesse ever could.

Noah swallowed, a tremor of fear crossing his face, and I realized just how nervous he was. He was barely holding it together against fear. And though mere inches separated our bodies, it felt like jumping from one galaxy to the next. It wasn't only about learning it. The true leap was in understanding that I needed to help him if either one of us was going to feel good.

And when that piece of the puzzle fell into place in my mind, I pulled my lower lip under my teeth and perked my ears. "Can I kiss you?"

"Fuck yes. Please." He closed his eyes as he answered me. His chin moved a little up and I leaned in, catching the sweet and citrusy scent of the American pale ale I'd ordered for him. The briefest pause in which my lips hovered over his felt like the longest, most excruciating wait of my life.

Every terrible outcome that had been so clear to me moments ago slipped away from my grasp.

An instant later, the chills of the February night were chased away by the searing heat of Noah's lips on mine. He was like the core of the Sun. His lips parted a little, as if by instinct, just as mine pressed against them. The sweetness of beer and victory mixed on my lips as I kissed him, my hands touching the sides of his torso, just above his hips. He kissed me back, if a little too eagerly, and our teeth touched for the briefest of moments. But I titled my head and took control over it, kissing him deeply and savoring the little moan that escaped from his mouth into mine. The corners of my lips stretched as I kissed him more, every little bit of me glimmering and vibrating, just like those electromagnetic forces he'd tried explaining to me. And just like they held atoms together, I held him. My unbreakable hold on him and his clutching of my jacket stranded us in each other's arms. We kissed softly, softer than I'd ever known to kiss, until the tip of his tongue ventured out in search of something more.

I was all too glad to provide it. My lips parted further and I pushed my tongue just far enough to meet his. And when they touched, the sparks burst to life. It was like all the suppressed lust I had tried shielding Noah from was unleashing. I found myself grappling against my own impulses. I wanted him. I wanted all of him all of the time and just to myself.

My tongue explored his mouth as he moaned over it and clutched my jacket harder. He wasn't letting me pull back even if such an outrageous thought crossed my mind.

I swirled us around, never letting my lips leave his, and pinned him against the intricately designed scrollwork of the iron post of the street lamp. He gasped, but resumed kissing me back with all the generous eagerness of someone who'd been dreaming of this for way too long.

It nagged me, somewhere deep in the back of my mind, that I was stealing his firsts, but I was so far gone in the passion of this moment that I couldn't pull myself back.

It just so happened that the virgin had more self-control than the player. He pulled his lower lip between his teeth and let out a small sound from his throat. "We should get warm."

And though I knew what the invitation was, even the idea of sitting in his room and listening to some new version of punk was too sweet to resist.

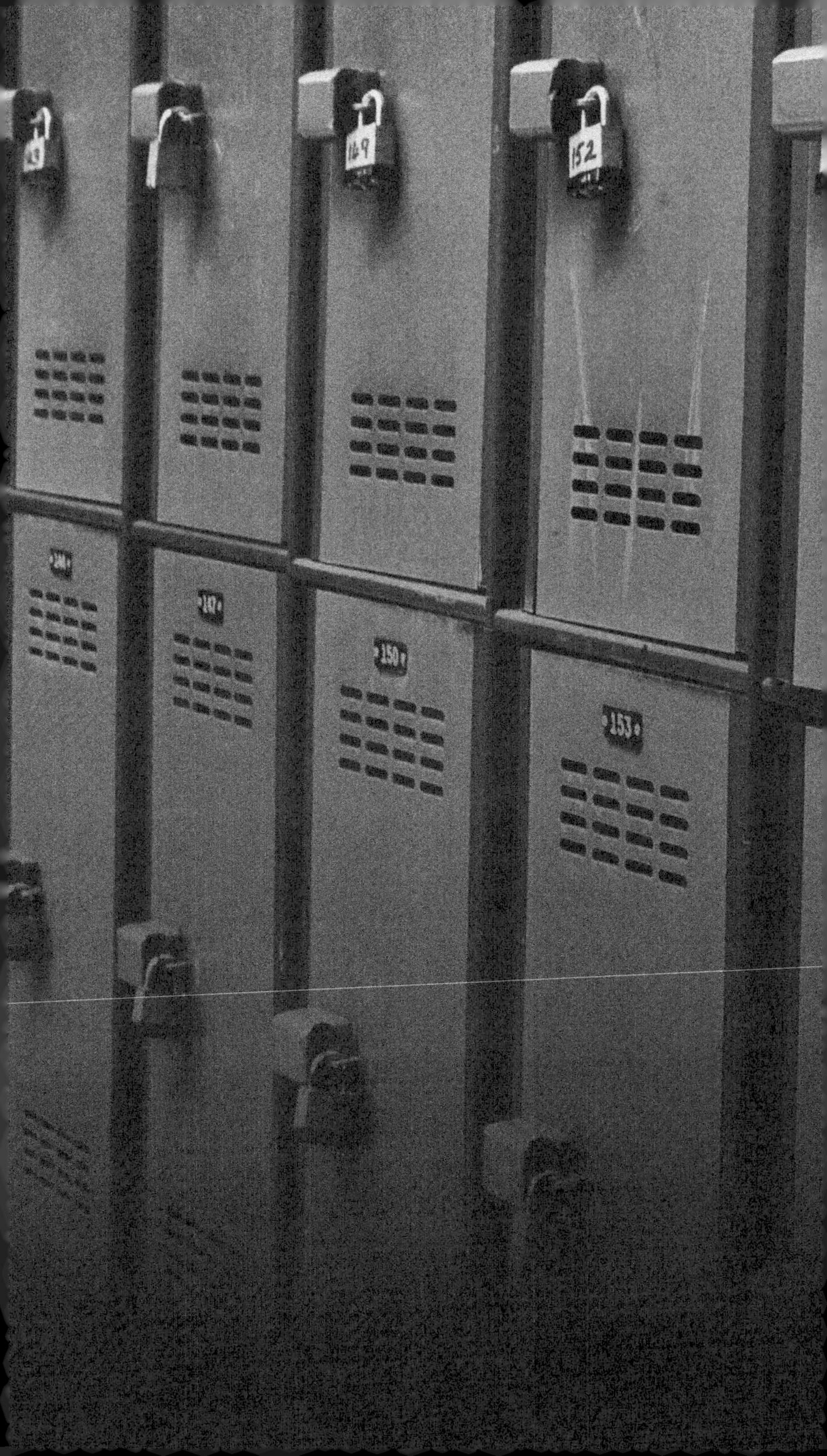
152
150
153

EIGHT

Noah

His lips were softer than I expected. All of him was like that. When I'd expected aggressive, I received caring. When I thought he would growl and grunt, he merely sighed. The broody bad boy was a sweetheart in disguise and the thought made my heart leap.

I kept biting my lip against the grins as we walked the rest of the way to my room. My insides were restless, stomach hollow, and groin tingling with excitement. He'd said yes to my invitation. Oh, and he'd kissed me like I'd never been kissed before.

My mind was swirling so fast it was risking escaping my head altogether.

Electrical currents raced through my body as I tried to walk like a normal human being, rather than an overexcited virgin about to punch his V-card.

I desperately wanted to snatch his hand and run off with him. This dating tutor was about to take the lessons to the next level. And when I thought of touching his bare hand with mine, tingles ran up my arm.

We walked in silence that was broken only by our

footsteps on the wet and frosty pavement and our quick breaths. My ears were flooded with my speeding heartbeat, too. The heat of our brief but sweet kisses was still running through my body, radiating from me, and threatening to cover me in sweat if we didn't undress soon.

"Finally," I muttered, the muscles in my face aching from all the force with which I was preventing goofy expressions. And now, when I glanced at Sawyer, who was keeping his serious face on, too, we let our gazes linger on one another.

He cracked first, his smile beaming with the intensity of a supernova, and I followed a fraction of a second later. Even biting my lip hard wasn't helping. My most excited smile stretched my mouth wide and I looked down. The tips of my ears heated.

I pushed into the dormitory building, then led the way upstairs to my room. My key was jingling in my hand as I tried and failed to unlock the door.

"Easy," Sawyer whispered. "Relax."

I can't believe that you like me, I wanted to say, but I changed my mind. It was wiser to stay silent than speak too soon. Still, he'd said it, and then he'd asked if he could kiss me. If anything had surprised me, it was the question. Sawyer seemed like the type of guy who kissed whoever he liked, assuming he was welcome because no one had ever said no to him.

My heart thumped hard in my chest as the key turned in the lock and we entered my room. The lower of the two switches turned the lamps and the Christmas lights around the room on. The heat of the broken radiator was more than I could bear in this state, but I didn't move to open the window. Instead, I tucked my hands into my pockets and stepped a little back from Sawyer.

He looked around, as though he'd never been here before, then fanned his face. "Still simmering," he said, then shrugged his black bomber jacket off and examined me carefully while hanging his jacket by the door. "Did I ever tell you how good blue and brown look on you?"

My ears pulled back as I grinned. This wasn't nearly as innocent as Sawyer commenting on my wardrobe as a dating tutor. This was a guy giving me a compliment. It was almost unheard of. "I don't think so," I said with a shrug, not because I wanted more compliments, but because I didn't want to lie to him again. Telling him the truth about being a virgin turned out to be the best damn thing I'd ever done.

"Well, the outfit is fire," he said. "Darker colors let your eyes glow."

I was about to wheeze. He stepped closer to me and I had a moment of utter imagination. My mind was filled with all the little glimpses of what I hoped for. My fingertips brushing against his skin. A sigh between our lips as our naked torsos touched. His hands everywhere on me. His cock...

I choked.

"Are you okay?" he asked.

I nodded. "Great."

He took a step back, then glanced at the shelf where my wireless speaker was. "Do you mind?" He slipped his phone out, signaling he would choose our music.

"Be my guest." I waited as he hooked up the speaker to his phone, then shuffled through his playlists. Classic rock filled the room moments later, although I didn't recognize the song. "I thought you were into more, erm, demonic music." I took my jacket off and hung it next to his.

He snorted and shook his head. "I am, but I'm a very diverse character."

"Mm." I was glad of the music because the silence would be heavy otherwise. My heart beat restlessly and my anxiety was spinning out of control. I had rarely wanted something this badly. And after all the little glimpses of Sawyer's personality — who am I kidding? His freaking amazing body, too — I finally dared to believe he was within my reach.

"Do you want to kiss me again?" he asked.

I admired the shameless confidence in the simple way he asked that question. He spoke it almost like he was asking me if I wanted the last bagel.

"Hell yeah." I breathed the words out and tensed as he approached me.

"It's okay to be nervous," he said, then nudged me to my bed.

My mind raced. Bed. Beds were where people had sex. Sex was what I wanted with Sawyer. Sawyer was here. Tonight. Willing. We were going to have sex. I was going to hyperventilate and faint.

But he was steady as we sat on the edge of the bed and turned to face each other. I wanted him to kiss me and sweep these thoughts away. I wanted him to take me and do *all* the things to me, so that I could finally graduate in life. So I would be free of this embarrassing cloud that followed me everywhere.

"We don't have to do anything more than make out," Sawyer said simply. "Not that I don't want to. Because, fuck, I can't believe you're into me." He was as open and free with words as I had ever seen him. "But if it's too much, we can do whatever you want."

At this point, I no longer knew where the heat was

coming from. It seemed to be everywhere. In the room, in me, in him, and in the space between us. A bare wire connected our bodies and the current made it blow.

I cleared my throat and looked into his eyes. "Listen," I said, my voice warning him not to be shocked. "I've been prepping the whole afternoon. If I don't have sex tonight I think I'll go crazy."

"Look at you," he said, half proud and half turned on, leaning in. "You just said sex without short circuiting."

I laughed and gently pushed his chest. It was a mere playful gesture, little more than a touch, but it opened the doors to a whole new reality. Sawyer recoiled from the push as though I'd punched him, then laughed and leaped at me, rolling me onto my back in a sweeping move, and wrestling his way on top of me.

I yelped and laughed, but his mouth on mine shut me up. His tongue found mine in an instant and my soul left my body. I drifted far beyond the confines of the room, then hurried back because I didn't want to miss a moment of him touching me.

He sprawled out on top of me, careless for my lack of air, and kissed me deeply until every inch of me was taut with expectation.

We grappled playfully, his hands wrapping around my wrists. I tried to break free of his hold as he bared his teeth, our sighs burst out of us in short and shallow breaths. I inhaled, wrenching my arms free of his hold, then fought back by digging my fingers into his ribcage and making him wiggle.

In all the years of watching adult actors move through their pretend foreplay, I had never seen a single one like this.

When I grabbed Sawyer's wrists, we glared at each other, faces flushed and bodies heating. "You're fighting a goalie, rookie," he growled, but he underestimated how hard I could cling to his arms and how long I could endure his wiggling. "You're so gonna lose."

"We'll see about that," I huffed, thrusting my hips up to tip him off balance. My crotch, already aching with the tightness of my pants, throbbed as it brushed against Sawyer's butt.

A chuckle erupted from him. "I felt that."

I would have been embarrassed in any other scenario but this. Mostly because the look of mischief covered Sawyer's handsome face as he sank down on me. He let all his weight press down on my bulge and my eyes rolled back in my skull. The sensation was such that it spread through my whole body, tension skyrocketing and my hands loosening around his wrists for just long enough that he could break free.

"I win," he announced shortly, then grabbed my arms again and lifted them all the way above my head, crossing my wrists and pressing his lips against mine.

If he wrestled with all his hookups, I didn't want to know. This felt like the only right way to do it. My hazy, lust-clouded mind couldn't come up with a less awkward transition between us sitting next to each other and full-on making out, mere moments apart. Every trace of anxiety was gone by the time his full, juicy lips covered mine.

I savored his kisses in case I never got them again. And I tucked my worries about that somewhere deep in the back of my mind. Would it come back and bite me in the ass? Probably. But I wasn't going to consider those paths now. Not when there was a hot keeper who wanted to bite my ass instead.

I shuddered at the thought and a whimper crossed from my lips to his. But Sawyer wasn't immune to it. A moan left him as he shifted his weight and his legs wiggled between mine, his crotch resting on top of mine, and our torsos pressing together. He was hard; I could feel it on my sensitive, throbbing cock.

"Those pants must be killing you," he said, his voice tight with lust and amusement.

"Uh-huh," I murmured. *Show some mercy. Take them off.*

I didn't know if he read these thoughts from my eyes or if it was simply the next logical step, but Sawyer kept one hand over my crossed wrists while sliding the other between us. The palm of his hand felt my bulge and I nearly cried out with joy.

How many times had I imagined this?

And yet, my imagination had failed miserably each and every time. The feeling was so much more packed with everything around us than I'd thought. It wasn't merely a hand touching my hard cock. It was a hand, but also his breath on my face and his heartbeat over mine, and the classic rock in the background, and the way the subdued lights kissed his face. The darkness of his eyes contracted against the glimmers of the lights reflected in them. The beautiful almond shape his eyelids formed left me short of breath and the arch his hair made over his face turned him into a contemporary deity. He was stunning in every way. And when he touched me, all these little thoughts converged until my lower back was arching in ecstasy and air was draining out of my lungs.

The ease with which he unbuckled my belt and undid

my button and zipper pointed to a well honed skill. A trace of jealousy zapped me, quickly covered by an immense sense of triumph that it was me he was undressing this night.

Sawyer allowed my pants to spread open over my crotch, but he didn't pull them down. Instead, he pecked my lips, then sat up on my legs to undo all of the buttons on my shirt. He was swift about it, fingers nimble and capable of doing intricate things with great ease. I wondered what else he could do with those fingers and the thought almost embarrassed me. It was as though my ability to feel any sense of shame was numbed by him kissing me so much.

As my torso bared, from the bottom button to the top, a glint of desire grew in Sawyer's eyes. He spread my shirt wide and bit his lip against smiling. When the moment passed, he set his hands on my chest and dragged them down my torso. "You need to show me your workout routine. It's doing you wonders."

I almost laughed, thinking he was teasing me. I was mostly flat, though the bench press Matt had forced me on broadened my chest and the ab coaster tightened my stomach. But as Sawyer traced every inch of my bare skin, I realized he wasn't kidding. This pleased look on his face was nothing short of genuine.

The sexy keeper liked me.

"Let me see you," I whispered, almost too nervous to ask, as though there was a chance he'd change his mind. I needed to remind myself that there was little I could do to blow it so badly — at least in this part — to make him run away. Whatever happened later, when the things I had no experience with began, would worry the Future Noah.

Sawyer did that thing with his lower lip, biting it and pulling it between his teeth. It made my dick throb and eyebrows arch. And when he started unbuttoning his shirt, I nearly lost it altogether. As he did it, I realized I had never seen him shirtless. At best, I had been stealing glimpses of his stomach when his tops pulled up by chance. But now, as he bared his torso, I placed every inch of him into my long-term memory.

He shrugged his shirt off, then unbuckled his belt and pulled it out of his pants, throwing both items on the floor behind him. One of his eyebrows quirked up. "Wanna touch me?"

"Fuck yeah," I breathed, thankful that he could read my face so well. He was chiseled, although thin for an athlete. Each muscle on his body was carved with precision, flowing smoothly from one to the next. His figure was a work of art and Sawyer was the artist. Each tattoo on his body screamed 'bad boy.' The large, gothic "Burn in Hell" was inked on his neck. A spiderweb covered one of his pecs and a blade seemingly sank into his heart. He was a canvas of edgy artwork. And when my fingertips grazed them, I blurted, "Did it hurt?" The fascination that I felt showed itself on Sawyer's face.

"Some hurt," he said simply. "But it was worth it." He covered my hands with his and pressed his own body harder, letting me get the full feel of his muscles and the relief of his figure. He dragged my hands from his collarbones all the way to his waist, then met my gaze. "Did that feel good?"

My throbbing cock answered the question for me.

"You can do whatever you want," he said, releasing my hands and starting to touch my abdomen. His hands felt their way to my neck. "I'll tell you if I don't like it."

His words were determined, albeit softened for the mood of the moment. "And you have to tell me if you don't like something, too."

I nodded.

"Promise." It was a crisp request that allowed for no debate.

I wondered why he insisted so much, but thought better than to discuss it. "I promise. I'll tell you."

"Good." And as soon as he said the words, he shifted and laid on top of me. His bare torso kissed mine while I let my hands follow the sides of his ribcage, then travel to his upper back, and trace his spine all the way down to the edge of his pants.

He was moving steadily, but perpetually. His cock, still trapped behind his pants, was pressing and pulling back from mine. The movements caught and pulled my pants a little, baring the tent of my underwear pitched by my merciless erection. Gasps and moans left my open mouth when Sawyer kissed my neck.

He'd told me I could try anything I wanted, but a huge obstacle in that was my conscious mind. I feared being told he disliked something. I feared him pulling back from me. But I was also dying to rest my hand on his bulge. I was desperate to slide it inside his pants and feel it throb over his underwear.

He kissed me softly down the length of my neck and along my collarbones, then up again to nibble on my earlobe. It made my body tingle and wiggle and empowered me to try things out. There were so many things that I wished to do. What would he taste like on my tongue? What would his lips around me feel like? Was he hairy or smooth? Would he let me suck his balls like I'd seen in porn? Would he rim me and finger me if I asked? Or was that something people never did in real life?

I hadn't even realized that my right hand was moving along the edge of his pants until I felt it slide between us. "Let me hold you," I whispered.

"Fuck yes," he said, practically into my ear.

Sawyer rolled off of me and onto his side, undoing the button and zipper on his pants and pulled them down a little to bare the big bulge in his blue boxer-briefs.

I held my breath as Sawyer moved his hand away and waited. My tongue moved over my lips as saliva filled my mouth and I swallowed. Turning to my right side to face him completely, I set my left hand on the middle of his chest and darted my eyes between his face and his crotch. When I breathed again, air flowed through my parted lips. I followed the center of his torso down to his underwear.

And when I reached the edge, there was no turning back. My hand gently wrapped around the thickness that stretched the blue fabric thin. Sawyer throbbed in my hand. "That feels so good," he said.

I was still gentle, almost fearfully so, as I stroked him.

"You can go harder," he said, moving his hand toward me to mimic what I was doing to him. When he set his hand on my bulge, I wanted to cry out again. Chills rose along my spine and I held my breath. My hips thrust forward by instinct, independent of my brain, and Sawyer gripped me firmly, applying pressure that forced my eyebrows to contort and lips to part wider. A strangled moan dragged through my throat and Sawyer grinned. "Like that?"

I nodded. It was painful in an odd, deeply pleasurable way. It wasn't even pain, but the pressure and the excruciating knowledge that I wanted more. I wanted him to slide his fist over my cock, free of my underwear.

I bit down on my lip hard and returned the favor. Sawyer frowned and stared into my eyes, stroking me firmly and wincing whenever his cock pulsed in my hand.

"Do you wanna take that off?" he asked.

I didn't know which part of my clothes he meant. I still wore my shirt, pants, and boxer-briefs with bananas stamped on them. So when I nodded, he released me to undress and I took a piece of clothing off one after the other. He watched me toss my pants off the bed, followed by my shirt. I then hooked my thumbs inside my underwear and pulled them over my cock and all the way down.

My heart raced twice as fast when my underwear fell off the bed. I was naked in front of a guy. In my bed. In my room. And his eyes were glowing with desire. He looked at my thick cock and swollen balls like it was all he wanted. He pressed his hand on my belly and dragged it all the way down until he felt the smoothness of freshly shaved skin around the base of my cock.

When I'd told him I'd spent the afternoon getting ready, I hadn't exaggerated. And when he inhaled through his teeth while feeling the smoothly shaved skin of my legs, I knew he appreciated my efforts.

His hand wrapped around the base of my cock and the fit of pulsing overtook me. Every little nerve ending in my body was aflame. I leaned in, lying on my side, and kissed him while running a hand through his hair. I had no idea where the thought came from, but I grabbed a fistful of hair on the back of his head and gripped it tightly, causing a smirk to stretch his lips.

Sawyer's kisses grew hotter and harsher against my lips. We made out sloppily and it turned me on so much more than I'd known was possible. Nothing in this exercise of passion was the way I'd expected. Every sensation I had ever given to myself paled into nothingness when compared to it. His hand was infinitely better at holding me than mine had ever been.

He stroked me gently, almost like he knew how taut and on edge I was. Maybe he did.

"Wait," I murmured against his lips. "Wait. I want to see you." I could feel him smiling against my mouth and face.

He released me from his grip and turned onto his back for long enough to slide his pants and underwear down. It was a sudden, graceless movement that made my heart leap with excitement. Holy fuck. He was long. I'd never been ashamed of my size, but Sawyer was both longer and thicker. At a solid eight inches, maybe a little more, he was equally intimidating as he was appealing.

He kicked his pants off and tucked his hands under his head. He lay on his back, naked, beautiful, heated. His cock was so stiff that it wasn't even lying on his body, but was at full mast. The slight curve in it made me wonder just how good it would feel inside of me and the thought made my stomach flutter.

I was biting my lip hard until I whispered, "Fuck, you look...so hot."

His ears perked just as I glanced up at him. It was odd to make eye contact while we were naked, but there was a familiarity between us that I hadn't thought existed until now. "Enjoy the view, sexy," he said, then heeded his own advice and let his gaze trail my entire body.

My heart stumbled and I set my hand on his leg. Hair was sparse on his thighs, although there was some on the lower half of his legs. It was soft under my fingers and fading into smooth skin the higher I reached. His balls, hanging heavy over his taint when he spread his legs a little, were smooth like mine, and a short-cropped patch of hair covered the skin above his cock.

The sweet scent that rose off of him was a mixture of his cologne, reminding me of spring and mountain ranges, and his natural musk. It was faint, but present and tickling all of my deepest desires.

I wasn't afraid of reaching for him and touching him. "You're so hard," I murmured.

"Yeah, I'm, uh…excited," he said and his voice matched the feeling he described.

I wrapped my fingers around his cock, the dark pink tip glistening with precum. Though I had never been this close to another person and had never even had a chance to do something like this, every instinct in my body told me to taste him. It felt like the most natural thing I could do. It felt like the most obvious wish.

"What if I suck at this?" I whispered as I scooted closer to him, stroking him slowly and licking my lips.

He snorted. "Sucking is kind of the idea."

That he could find humor in a situation that was as tense as this relaxed me as much as if he'd lifted the burdens with his bare hands.

"Do you wanna try it?" he asked. His abs tensed and he rose to a half-sitting position.

I nodded, looking up at him.

His hands closed around my face and he leaned in to kiss me softly for a little while. When he moved back, I was ready for whatever he wanted to do. And I was braver than ever before. I wanted him. In my mouth and in my throat. I wanted his scent on my lips, his flavors on my tongue. I wanted all of it, right now.

"Um...tell me if I'm..." I didn't know what.

He nodded solemnly. "You'll do fine, Noah. Relax." And as he dragged himself higher along the bed, he set my pillow to support his back. I moved over simultaneously, so that I lay on my front between his legs. This felt natural to me and Sawyer didn't protest.

He would tell me.

His legs spread a little wider and I scooted closer to his crotch, giving in to the sudden urge to kiss his thigh and trace it all the way to his groin. There, I felt his cock against my cheek, and nearly suffered a heart-attack when lust drilled through my chest.

He groaned as he exhaled and I turned my head around so that my lips were following the length of his cock. His throbs were evident against my mouth as I reached the tip of his cock. There, I lingered a moment, remembering this so that I could pull the memory whenever I wanted it for the rest of my life.

And then, with nothing else in the universe seeming more appealing than this, I parted my lips and lowered my head onto his cock. The sensations were instant and explosive. The sweet-and-salty flavor of his precum didn't surprise me as much as the soft texture of his skin and the intensity of the throb that filled my mouth.

"Tss. Easy on the teeth," Sawyer said, humor touching his voice.

I pulled my head up and looked at him, mortified. "Sorry."

"Don't be. You didn't bite it off. Just go easy." He was so casual, almost like he was showing me how to lick a lollipop.

And as soon as the thought crossed my mind, I felt my tongue stretching out of my mouth and pressing against the lower side of his cock. I used my hand to keep him in place and dragged my tongue all the way up to the tip. The shudder and long exhale coming from Sawyer told me I'd struck gold.

When my tongue reached the very tip of his cock, I closed my lips around it and sucked it in. Making sure my lips protected him from my teeth, I gently bent my head down and felt him fill me. I didn't know how much of him I had taken, but I knew my limit as soon as I reached it.

"Slowly, slowly," Sawyer was whispering. "Relax. It gets easier."

I heeded his advice, oddly encouraged that his infinite patience with me allowed me to explore my own limits as well as his. And just like he'd said, I moved my head back and forth slowly until I realized that every few moves, his cock was settling deeper in my mouth. It rubbed the roof of my mouth, but it also dipped into my throat. The first time I lowered myself that far, the muscles in my throat tightened and cut off the flow of air that had already been irregular. But Sawyer placed his hands on my face and lifted my head a little, letting me breathe, before he moved his hips and impaled my head on his cock.

"Fuck, that feels good," he murmured. I wasn't sure if he was only saying it to make me feel better or if I was doing something right. Regardless, I kept my lips sealed and my tongue gently pressing the underside of his cock. The trick I didn't know how to master was relaxing my throat, but that didn't seem to bother Sawyer. He knocked his dick into my mouth again and again, his abs flexing under one of my hands, his grunts like music in my ears.

I found myself restlessly grinding against the

mattress. His dick filled my mouth, but it didn't do all the things I was dying for. It only hinted at them. It only made me want them more. It was delicious and sexy, but I needed to be closer to him. My chest was tightening with this urgent need and I rubbed my crotch mercilessly against the bed, whimpering over his dick every now and then.

When Sawyer throbbed three times in rapid succession, he stopped his movements abruptly. "Fuck, Noah," he groaned and nudged my head away. And, when our eyes met, he repeated in slightly more than a whisper, "Noah."

I licked my lips, then licked them again. My brain swam far away from me, my mind in tatters. I couldn't believe I had him in my bed, naked and ready for anything. "Are you gonna fuck me, Sawyer?" I asked, almost tripping over the word.

A grin spilled across his face and he cupped my cheeks, then pulled me by the head to kiss my lips. I wore his scent without shame and felt him smile against my lips as he kissed me deeper. "If you want me to," he said after he pulled back an inch from my mouth.

"Please. I'll die if you don't." The humor drained out of my tone and the statement sounded almost like a promise, but Sawyer chuckled anyway.

I felt him find his cock and stroke it gently. "We can't have that." He pecked me again, then again, and again. "Lie like that," he said as he shifted and pulled away from me, then showed me how to position myself.

My elbows sank into the mattress, propping up the top half of my torso. My head lowered, my brow resting on my folded hands. The pressure on my hard cock was nearly unbearable as I let the rest of me lie flat on the bed, legs spread so that Sawyer could nestle himself between them.

I held my breath as Sawyer knelt behind me, then allowed his body to fit perfectly against mine. His chest rested on my upper back, his stomach fit into the curve of my lower back, his cock nestled between my cheeks and his balls hanging down my taint. His legs followed mine and his head was to my right. When he kissed me, shivers ran down my arms.

I didn't know what he was doing. I'd expected him to probe me, feel me, and finally help me shed my virginity. Instead, Sawyer was kissing my ear and neck, then my upper back, then all the way down my spine.

When I realized what he was up to, he was already down on the small of my back, hands cupping my butt and making me shudder with the sensation. I'd never realized it could feel so good to be touched so intimately. Porn, for what it was good for, had a great many limitations. And the sense of closeness to another human was the biggest one.

Sawyer gripped my cheeks and spread them, his hot breath washing over my most intimate parts. "Ready?" Even the vibration of his voice felt like we were making love already. In a way, we were. These things were far less clear-cut when you were doing them. Surprisingly to a virgin with expectations, I felt so intimately tied to Sawyer whenever his skin met mine. Oh, but I wanted more of him. I wanted all of him.

"Uh-huh," I hummed and gasped as soon as his lips touched me where no one had ever been. My hole tightened with nervousness and my mouth dropped open, although no sound left me. I breathed freely, my throat open to let the air flow. My breaths grew shorter in an instant as warm wetness spilled over my hole and spread through my entire body. I didn't know which sensation was literal and which was a pure figment of my imagination, but they merged and splashed against my insides, welling in me like a rising tide. His smooth face buried between my cheeks, Sawyer licked me gently, then harsher and faster. Yes, he was careful with me. As careful as if I were made of the thinnest layers of glass. But he treated me as an adult, too. There was nothing condescending about this. He didn't shield me from feeling how far our desires could take us.

He ate me, his kissing and sucking messy, almost sloppy. His breaths were growing hotter and faster against my bare skin. And, every so often, he would shock me with his words. "You taste so fucking good," he said and made me blush. Then, some moments later, he said, "I knew you'd be delicious. I fucking knew it."

If I had any wits about me, I would have been happy that he had considered that at all. But I was far too gone to form opinions.

I let my torso flatten over the bed and moved my hands back to cover his on my cheeks, pulling them apart together for his magic tongue to work wonders. He licked me all the way from my taint, over my rim, and above. He let the tip of his tongue circle my hole, then pressed it hard against my entrance as if he wanted to reach inside of me.

The novelty of the sensation made me tighten all of my muscles. I shivered and rubbed my face against the pillow, desperately enduring the sweetest torment of my rising needs. "God...please..." My words were split and strangled. "Sawyer..."

"Mm." He hadn't even moved an inch away from me.

The sound left his nose and vibrated against my butt, his tongue working slickness into me. And when he did move, he asked me the hottest thing I'd ever heard spoken to me. "Can I finger you?"

"Fuck yes," I whispered, letting his right hand slide from under mine. I kept my cheeks spread for him, my head sinking deeper into the pillow. I moved my hips slowly, rubbing my cock against the bed and my own body. But when Sawyer touched me, I froze.

"It's okay. I'll go easy," he said soothingly.

I had used my finger more times than I could count, as well as a few toys that would never see the light of day and which lived in a box in my closet. I knew the techniques and all there was to expect. But when Sawyer massaged my hole, all that knowledge fell out of my head and I merely moaned, briefly harmonizing with the song that was currently playing from my speaker.

A drop of heated saliva fell onto my hole, just where Sawyer was touching me, and he gave it a little rub, firmer now. As if he could feel me relax — and he probably could — his finger slipped into me as soon as my muscles allowed it. I closed up immediately, but an inch of his finger remained inside of me.

A moan that dragged out of me was something I'd never heard myself do. It was both pained and dripping with pleasure. It was needy and slutty, desperate for Sawyer to proceed.

His finger remained where it was until I could breathe a little freer again. I forced my hole to open for him and Sawyer pressed on, filling me carefully and licking the rim from above.

Although the sensation wasn't something particularly unusual, it was vastly different from doing this same thing by myself. I didn't have the foresight as I would when I controlled my own hand. I needed to trust Sawyer and that was the defining difference between the two.

I trusted him.

Whether he would push himself deeper or pull out a little, it didn't matter, so long as I trusted him to find the best way. And he did. Gently, he filled me with one finger until he couldn't go deeper, but he wasn't forcing anything. Instead, he began to move his hand back and forth, getting me used to the sensation that I craved so much.

"You're so fucking horny, aren't you?" Sawyer said, his voice hoarse with lust.

My hips thrust back in reply, forcing him to finger me harder. When he added another finger, I grunted into the pillow against the odd sensation of my hole being stretched. It wasn't exactly painful. There was a great deal of pleasure tacked onto the physical impulses which my brain didn't know how to decipher. Pride, accomplishment, fear. Somehow, all these things existed at once.

"I can't," I whimpered, choking. "Harder. Please."

Sawyer placed his left hand on the small of my back, making it bow in, then rammed his two fingers deep into my body, filling me and making my cock throb violently when he pressed against my prostate.

The searing heat spread through me and I tensed all my muscles with the sole aim to relax my entrance for him. As I did, precum tickled my cock as it leaked. Sawyer abandoned all reservations, thrusting his fingers into me and pulling them out until friction warmed my hole.

My toes curled, my stomach fluttered, and my hole was in a perpetual state of delicious torment that I didn't know how to describe any other way. His skillful movements were so much more than I had done to myself. There had always been a level of hesitation in me, not going that extra mile. I'd never pushed my body to the limits. I'd never had the self-control to postpone my orgasm in order to explore myself like this. But Sawyer didn't care if I was dying to come. He was edging me another way altogether. He strung me tight and spread me thin. He stretched me loose and spat on my hole to wet me on the inside. The sloppy sound of his fingers ramming into me and sliding out might have embarrassed me with anyone else, but the deep purrs from Sawyer cued me into his own pleasures.

"Fuck me, please," I begged. "Fuck me already."

"Oh yeah," he rasped, shoving his fingers all the way in, then twisting his hand so that I felt every little tingle dispersed inside my body like blood distributed oxygen. "You're ready."

He pulled his hand out, then nudged me to turn onto my back. As I did, I found that he was somehow even harder now. His cock was stiff, almost darker than it had been a few minutes ago, as blood filled it to bursting. It was wet with both my saliva and his precum, which made my own cock glossy and slick, too.

I caught my breath and watched Sawyer as he lifted his pants from the floor and slid out a small square pack. It was telling that my dating coach was always prepared, but I filed that thought away. Instead, I watched him rip the foil wrapper with his teeth and slip the condom on easily. "Got lube?" he asked.

I cleared my throat, then leaned over the side of the bed to the bottom drawer of my nightstand. There, a small tube was half-spent, and I noticed Sawyer smirk a little as I handed it to him. "What?" I asked, playfully accusing.

"I'd love to see what else this room hides," he said.

I shot him a curious look, trying to seem mysterious.

Then, Sawyer said the two words that made my heart leap and bang against my ribcage. "Next time." And with that, he was quiet, pouring lube onto his fingers generously, slathering it over his hard cock, then bringing the excess to my butt. His fingers caressed me so gently between my cheeks as I lay on my back that I wished to cry out and beg him to take me, fuck me, and shred me to bits.

He raised his eyebrows and I nodded.

"Stay like that," he said before I even attempted to turn around. "I want to look at your face when I enter you."

Strangled, I gave up on breathing and simply spread my legs. *I'm yours to enter. I'm yours to play with and do with however you please. Use me.* But words, though welling, wouldn't form on my lips.

Instead, I surrendered myself to the current of passion that Sawyer was. He lifted my legs, then grabbed my second pillow and tucked it under the small of my back. "There. That's better," he murmured as he worked on my comforts. He took my ankles and bent me over until my bare feet rested on his hard pecs. Then, he leaned in, balling me so that my knees neared my shoulders. My butt-cheeks spread for him and I made my muscles push my rim to relax and accept him.

Sawyer looked into my eyes, matching my expectant gaze and biting his lip just like I did. It felt as though he was slowing everything down so I could remember it exactly. And when the tip of his cock touched my hole, a whimper loaded in my chest. I held it as it inflated and ascended.

We both held our breaths as Sawyer eased himself into me. A choked moan broke out of my throat and he stopped, though not even an inch inside, and pulled out. His hand, which had been holding his cock steady, rubbed and soothed me. Then, careful as before, he tried again only to feel me clench around his head hard and bite his lip. A half-laugh left him as he pulled back, then nodded at me to go again.

This time, I used every trace of stubbornness I could call to the surface. I forced myself to remain open for him, relaxed and loose. He'd prepared me better than I had ever done with any toy I'd ever used. I could do this.

And though the feeling was all different than with a rubber dildo, his thickness felt absolutely perfect inside of me. The first inch filled me, then the second, and the tension I had been feeling lifted as if we had brought down a dam. I felt invincible after an instant. The sensation came fully and at once. This was it.

Sawyer was inside of me. Sawyer was so close to me that our bodies were mashing together.

I was no longer a virgin.

As I exhaled a shuddering breath of air, Sawyer leaned into me further, filling me with half his length before pulling a fraction back. He nodded approvingly. "That's a good boy." And, as those words did something to my heart, he thrust his hips forward and entered me deeper.

It took several more moves, each making me feel stronger and bigger and better at everything, before I felt his abdomen and balls grind against me.

"Oh fuck," he moaned, fucking me deep, although he was still slow and steady about it. "Does that hurt?"

I took a second to decide. "No." It was just as before. This wasn't pain. This was a feeling I welcomed wholeheartedly even if some part of it resembled discomfort. That discomfort was soon fading, giving way to the absolute pleasure and sense of appropriateness.

He nodded at my answer, then leaned in until my feet slipped off his chest and my legs bent over his shoulders. This way, when he continued leaning, his destination was easily reached. His lips met mine and he kissed me as his hips jerked back and forth, kicking moans out of me and him together. Our voices and our breaths merged together as we made out, his cock impaling me and rubbing hard against my prostate.

If I had thought I would come at the first touch of another guy, I had underestimated a lot of things. The tension of my muscles, there to keep me relaxed by sheer force, also kept my dick from throbbing. But the welling feeling of a nearing orgasm was present nonetheless. It was rising with each swing of Sawyer's hips.

I placed my hands on his hips and followed his motions. Simply feeling his bare skin under my fingertips was enough to make me dizzy. And as our passion grew more heated and as sweat covered our bodies, I lost control of my limbs. I found myself crying out with joy and pleading for more, slapping his hard chest with my hands and enjoying every little move he made.

When Sawyer moved my legs off his shoulders so he could spread them apart and fuck me while kneeling straight and upright, I discovered I could be hornier still. He towered, gorgeous and handsome, built so finely and shining with a thin layer of sweat. He filled me under the angle that made my prostate his main destination, rubbing against it with each thrust.

And each time, a little more precum pooled in my belly button, the itching need for the climax growing.

I wanted him to do this all night, yet I was desperate for my orgasm.

"Please," I grunted, barely in control of my tongue. "I need to…"

"You're so close," Sawyer whispered, thrusting himself into me and kicking breaths of air out of my lungs. And when he swiped his hand over my cock, every little bit of me tensed. I felt myself clenching around the base of his thickness. His cock penetrated me harder, the sensation spreading faster and further to my curling toes and fingers. His hand gripped me as I throbbed and air stopped flowing into me.

In the ecstasy of pleasure, I managed to cry out a moment before my cock sent spurts of my hot wetness all over my bare stomach and chest. My abs tensed without a moment to relax and I looked at Sawyer's gorgeous face as he opened his mouth and released an airy moan. "Fuck," he whispered, lips barely moving, before his cock jerked ferociously inside of me.

Sawyer filled the condom, fucking me ruthlessly for a minute longer, as tingling soared through my entire body. I was so spent and satisfied that I could have fallen asleep the moment he leaned in and covered my body with his. I wrapped my arms around his bare torso, feeling his sticky, sweaty skin on mine, his heated body glowing just like mine was. I inhaled, my heart pounding quickly against his chest.

"Th-thank you," I whispered, running a hand through his hair on the back of his head.

I could feel him smile in the crook of my neck. "Fuck, Noah," he murmured. "You don't have to thank me for this. It was..." His voice trailed off for a moment, my guts wrenching in expectations. "Beautiful," he finished decisively as he relaxed, his cock sliding all the way out of me with ease, warmth of both friction and passion lingering behind.

A couple minutes later, Sawyer got up. I moved, but he waved for me to stay as I was. He snuck into the bathroom, then returned after disposing of the condom. He carried a towel with a bit of it soaked under hot water, then wiped the mess I had made on myself. He was careful and gentle like it gave him pleasure to do this.

I abruptly had the strongest urge to pull him in and hold him until he realized I wasn't letting go. I wanted to keep him here all night long. I wanted him to surrender himself to all the ways in which I could make him feel nearly as good as he had made me.

When I was clean, Sawyer scanned me and gave an approving nod, smiling to himself. "There you go."

He went into the bathroom again and I closed my eyes. My heart kept tripping as I tried to make my brain understand that it was over. I had done it. I was no longer a virgin.

I suppose the real feeling would sink in later. Right now, all I was thinking about was the bliss Sawyer had left in me. And when he returned, he was still unashamedly naked, as if putting his underwear on was an unthinkable act. He lay on the bed like he owned it, scooted against me, and sighed with the sort of tranquility I had never heard from him. "How do you feel?" he asked, locking our gazes together.

"I..." I didn't know how to pour the feelings into thought, then translate those thoughts into words. I felt like the world was no longer the same. I felt like I had just closed a chapter in my life. It was like being a traveler who had just returned from exploring uncharted territory. This was the place in which it had all begun, but I was no longer the same. I was better and wiser and more adult with the experience. "I feel amazing," I said, too far gone in my dreaming to repeat any of the words that had crossed my mind. "You made me feel amazing."

Sawyer bit his lip and nodded. "Me too."

And my heart nearly exploded in my chest. The spark of mischief in his eyes was overshadowed by the pure, unfiltered longing that radiated out of him. He was honest. He was saying that because he wanted me to know and not because he was polite.

It took effort to resist the urge to pull him in and hold him so tightly that he couldn't breathe. I didn't want to come across as a pathetic, clingy guy who was desperate for attention right after losing his virginity.

But Sawyer wasn't a clingy guy and he had lost his virginity a long time ago. So, when he wrapped his arms around me and pulled me in so hard that our bodies nearly melted into one another, my heart wanted to break out of my chest and my stomach was filled with butterflies taking flight.

He kissed my cheek, then my lips, and I realized how little I had expected of this. I hadn't gone so far as to imagine what it would look like to lie in bed after sex, but to be kissed was a surprise. Had I given it any thought, I would have discovered that my expectation was to be left alone.

I very much preferred what Sawyer was doing.

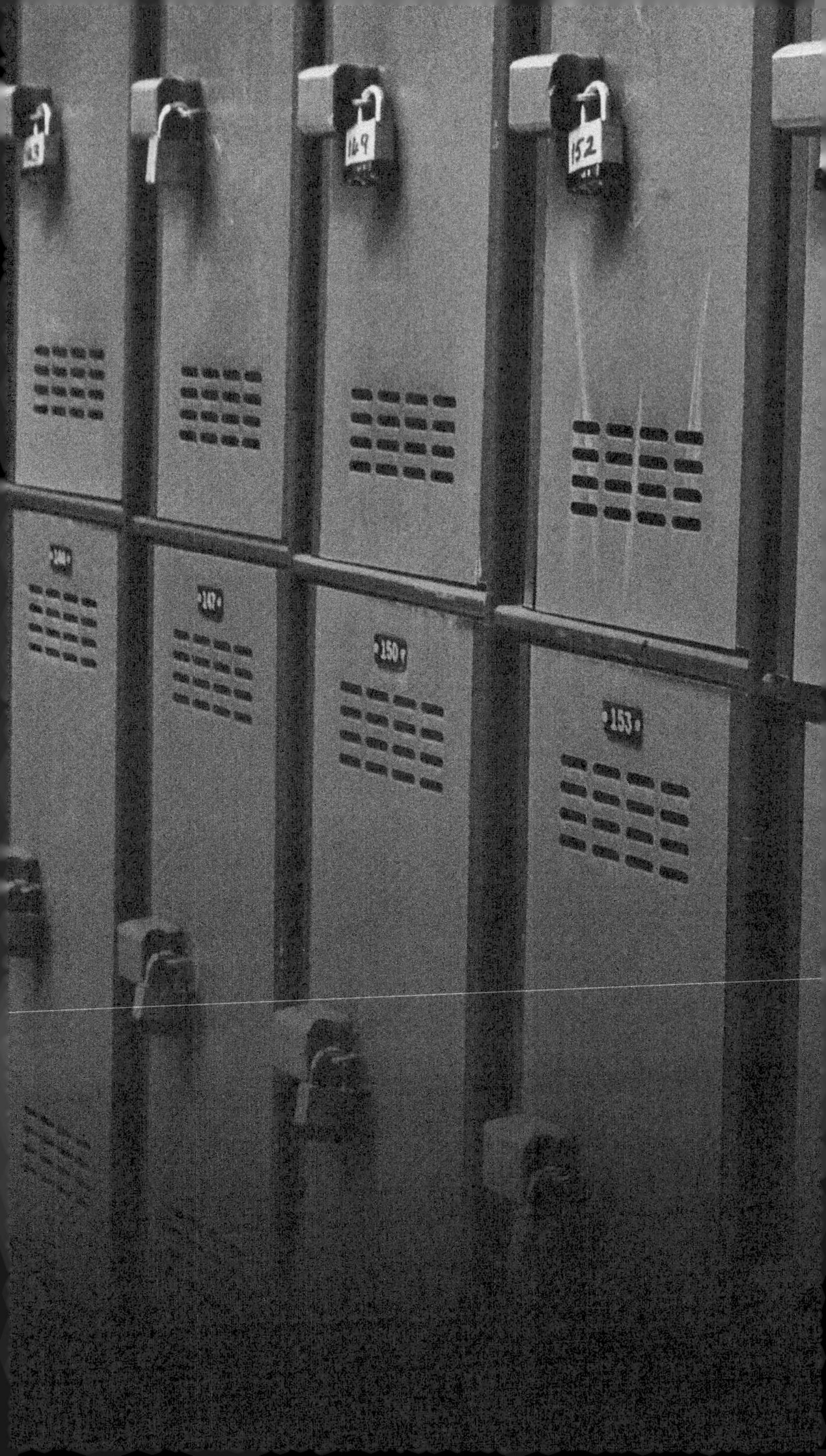
152
150
153

NINE

Sawyer

ALTHOUGH WE HAD A LATE START ON SATURDAY morning and I had gotten plenty of opportunity to explore every line and curve and shadow of his torso with my fingertips as he dipped in and out of tranquil sleep, my head was still filled with Noah as I headed back to the house. It was especially so because of the kiss at his door on my way out. He had seemed so uncertain whether to try for it or not. Like last night, he had desperately begged for it with his eyes and the teeth holding his lower lip, then was genuinely surprised when I took his shoulders in my hands and stilled him for a deep and passionate kiss.

I had left Noah blushing and decided it was the wisest to try for a date test once again before letting him pass. The first round was way too much fun to leave it at that. But for the second, I had grander ideas.

It was only unfortunate that the second date wouldn't happen for at least another week. Already at our morning practice, Coach Murray announced schedule changes for our matches. And if that wasn't bad enough, the locations rotated, too. And, as Saturdays went, I was busy with conditioning in the afternoon, and then writing up an essay for World Literature, which was a drag. It wasn't until nine in the evening that I succeeded at peeling myself off the desk chair in my room.

"Staying the night again?" Avery asked. The flat and expressionless tone he used hid the coy and teasing sting well, but not well enough. I knew better than to take Avery the way he presented himself.

I snorted and scanned the almost curious twinkle in Avery's eyes. "I'm only going for a walk." Somehow, telling anyone, even my best friend, about Noah felt like sacrilege. He had trusted me to be his first. He had practically asked me for help in stepping over that invisible threshold. And no matter how common it was for Avery and I to brag to each other in passing, I couldn't do it when it came to Noah.

"Alright, keep your secrets," Avery teased. His gray eyes seemed to hold knowledge he had no way of possessing.

"No secrets here, buddy," I insisted. "You should know that by now."

Avery pressed the tip of his finger against the side of his nose. "Don't I know it."

I swallowed a laugh and went out. The conversation, however brief, was on my mind as I crossed the blocks between the house and the dormitories. This wasn't the only thing that felt different when it concerned Noah. Last night, when we'd been together, every shred of my being was on alert. I hadn't wanted him to be in pain. I hadn't wanted him to experience even the slightest discomfort. And though he hadn't cared for anything but to be done with it, I wanted him to be able to look back on it with something other than a shudder or embarrassment. And he had been perfect. He had been so wonderful that I couldn't get him out of my head.

And that sensation was new to me.

There was a small part of me that felt deep shame at admitting this. The best excuse I could offer was that I didn't know any better, but that was already a slippery slope. In truth, it was pretty inexcusable. I had never before put the other person's needs before mine. I had never before been in a situation where it felt like I definitely needed to. But with Noah, I had known, instantly, that my sole purpose was to show him there was nothing scary and terrible about it. Initially, I had put my own enjoyment aside. I had intended for him to have the best time, regardless of my rising passion and desire for rough play that was more than inappropriate for a virgin's first time.

And then, pure magic happened.

In the end, I had enjoyed myself so much more, despite the effort to show him what lovemaking was all about and to avoid my not-so-tame cravings.

When I found myself knocking on his door, my heart tripped. I was leaning against the doorframe, my left arm bent a little above my head. The footsteps were as swift as ever and I already expected to find him wearing little more than his underwear in the sweltering heat.

"Hey, cutie," I said as he opened the door, then decided not to cringe at myself. He was, genuinely, cute. His hair was messy and his glasses were perched on the tip of his nose. His cheeks were red, complementing his green eyes, but he was also fully dressed. And he had company.

Noah's eyes widened. "Be right back, Jake," he said, then shut the door behind his back and found himself safely pinned against it. I let my weight press against him as I leaned in and kissed those juicy red lips. After that, he took a moment to inhale and blinked fast a few times. "I wasn't expecting you."

"Sorry. I wasn't thinking. Of course, you're all booked up." I didn't let my disappointment show. This wasn't about me, for once. "I just wanted to see you."

Something almost like a chuckle left him, except it sounded too similar to an excited squeal. "That's okay."

So, I looked at him. I took all of him in. His scents, his warmth, his flavors. I kissed him one more time, then decided to do what I had come for. Well, one of the things I had come for. "So, I had a schedule change," I said. "We're doing a scrimmage tomorrow night, then we're off to Chicago for a charity game before our match there against the *Northern Wolves*. I thought I'd be here until Wednesday, and I won't be back until Friday."

"Um..." Noah's brow creased. "Okay."

And it hit me as abruptly as if someone had snuck up on me and struck the back of my head with an iron skillet. He didn't expect me to keep him looped in. But, as I considered this and reminded myself of all his pleased sighs this morning while we had been making out, I also understood why he had no expectations of me. He simply didn't believe I would tell him where I was and when I was free. We didn't have that kind of relationship.

I cleared my throat and cracked a smile. "So, if you're free on Saturday, I'd like to hang out. And if you're not..." I pushed into him, pinning him against the door once more, and leaned in to whisper into his ear. "You better reschedule whoever's keeping you busy."

Noah instantly shuddered and reached to hold the side of my torso. "Fuck. Yes. Okay. I'm free on Saturday."

"Good," I said, pulling back from him with a grin on

my face. I was ridiculously happy we had another date. "I didn't want to leave before telling you where I was. I didn't want you getting ideas. After all, you are an overthinker."

He chuckled and shook his head.

"You are," I insisted. "So, there you have it. I'll leave you to this Jake person now. He better be worth it."

His fingers dug deeper into the soft spot above my hip. Like a kitten who still wanted to play, he held onto me, then smiled and reluctantly released me. "Saturday."

"Saturday." It was a promise. And I sealed that promise with another kiss that made my heart beat faster than any kiss had managed to in years.

Noah's gentle moan met mine and I pinned him harder against the door. Every part of me tingled with excitement as if I hadn't done this with another person a million other times. I shivered with a desperate desire to hold him a moment longer. It was so strong and sudden that I couldn't even help but grin while kissing him.

He never moved. He never protested. Instead, his hands moved from the sides of my ribcage to the top of my chest. He kissed me back just as intently, the sweet flavor of his lips accented by the awkward reservation that battled his eagerness. The two clashed and made him such a unique boy to kiss that I found my heart jittered more, not less, as time went on.

The back of Noah's head faintly bumped against the door. My hands searched his body, feeling every inch of him until I cupped his butt and squeezed him so hard that he moaned over my lips.

Suddenly, the door flew open and we nearly tumbled into his room, separating in the leap. Noah cleared his throat and heat flushed my face as we straightened ourselves. There, an equally horrified Jake stared between us. "Sorry, I thought...you knocked."

Noah murmured something about everything being fine, his voice rising into a squeal by the end of the sentence, and I bit my lip against bursting into laughter. "I'll see you later," I said and turned on my heels.

"Okay." It was a whisper so drenched in the expectation that I wanted to take him right away. But I couldn't. He was busy being a genius and all that. And I needed to get ready for a surprise trip to Chicago.

But, life kicked in, and my heart kept tripping at every thought of the next weekend. The things I wished to do to him. The things I wanted him to experience. I was more inspired than ever before. That was probably why this week began to drag as soon as I was away from Noah.

The trip seemed longer than it was possible, according to the rules of physics that governed the passage of time. And once there, the only good thing I could hold onto was hockey. We played a mean game for a good cause, filling the arena to its maximum capacity, and scoring a blazing victory on our first night there. The spirits were high among us.

After we returned to our hotel rooms, I pulled out my phone and began a text that got away from me. By the time I typed out the impressions of the night, I realized it was a mile long. *Pathetic*, something told me, so I erased the wall of text and substituted it with a short and sweet one.

Me: Victory is ours.

Noah's reply came a few excruciating minutes later. I'd already begun to believe he had no idea what I was talking about. After all, he didn't exactly need to pay attention to the things I was doing outside our tutoring sessions.

Noah: Celebrating tonight?

Noah: I mean, you don't have to tell me.

Noah: I don't mean, you know, 'celebrating' but like, are you going out for drinks?

Noah: Fuck. Ignore me. Long day.

Me: You're seriously overthinking this. And for what it's worth, I'm in a bathrobe on my bed, waiting for room service and calling it early tonight.

Avery was humming to himself in the bathroom while I grinned at my phone and waited for Noah's reply. Just then, Avery came out of the bathroom in a cloud of cologne. "What the hell?" he asked, his surprise limited to the slightest quirk of his eyebrows.

"What?" I asked, glancing at my phone. I found nothing there, then put it on the nightstand.

"I thought we were going out, dude," Avery said, sitting down on the edge of his bed. "We're away. It's what we do."

He was right. Whenever we'd been at away games — and especially when we were the victors — Avery and I would hit the town the way only two best wingmen and friends would. "Ah, I'm kinda tired," I said, reaching for my phone and checking if there were notifications. There were none.

"Right," Avery said. Something about his tone told me he didn't buy it. It was just that Avery's normal and sarcastic voices were so alike that you could never be totally sure.

I snorted. "We've been in Chicago a dozen times, dude. You're not gonna get lost."

"No, but I thought we were going out together," Avery said, giving a little shrug.

I cocked my head to the side. Was he doing an... emotion? I didn't know how to deal with one if he was. "Look at it this way. Without me in the picture, you're gonna be the most desirable bachelor there."

Avery's skeptical look tickled me. "You only ever had more luck, buddy." His lips trembled in the corners like he was about to smile. "Come on. Spill the truth. What's keeping you here?"

I shrugged. "I told you. I'm just tired."

"And yet, you look as alert as if we're still on the ice. Spill it, Sawyer." He leaned a little forward while all my gestures closed. I crossed my legs and my arms. "Fuck, dude. You've totally lost it for that guy, haven't you?"

If I didn't know better, I'd think my robot friend was smirking. "I don't know what you're talking about."

Avery narrowed his eyes. My phone dinged. Avery's eyes shot wide open and he actually stretched his sharp lips into a wolfish grin. "Your boyfriend's calling," he said.

"What?" I asked, my voice airy and heat rising to my face. "We're not boyfriends. He's not...my... You know what? Shut up."

Avery threw his head back and laughed out loud. "I didn't think I'd ever see the day."

"What day?" I blurted, staring in terror at this laughing person who possessed my best friend's body. "This isn't the day. You won't see the day. You're acting weird."

Avery nodded and got up. "Chill, dude. Your secret's safe with me." Then the fucker winked and turned away from me.

As Avery walked toward the door, I murmured after

him. "It's not a secret. There's no secret. I don't even know what you think I'm hiding."

He exhaled shortly, which, in Avery's language, was laughter, and shook his head. "Suit yourself. And say hi to your lover boy." He glanced at me over his shoulder, his gray eyes sparkling, then marched out of the room.

I needed a moment to compose myself before lifting my phone. It wasn't my secret to tell. Besides, we'd only hooked up once, so it wasn't something I wanted to advertise.

But there lay the problem, too. Avery and I, for better or worse, didn't keep these things secret from one another. We talked plainly about these things and, it shamed me to admit, even bragged about our escapades.

The fact that I wasn't doing it now gave Avery all sorts of wrong ideas.

But it felt unholy to do it to Noah. I wasn't going to tell anyone about him if he didn't approve first.

Just as I was lifting my phone, a knock on my door alerted me that my food had arrived. After room service left I checked the contents of the platter, wrinkled my nose at it, and realized that it wasn't food I was ravenous for. I left the little cart where it stood and returned to my phone.

Noah: Did you say you were in your bathrobe?

He sent a drooling emoji after that, then an embarrassed one, then an apology if he overstepped my boundaries. He was still overthinking it and I decided enough was enough. Without another thought, I spread the bathrobe open to bare my chest, then sent Noah a selfie.

Me: Enough proof?

I was chuckling to myself until a message came back.

Noah: Enough? Never. The evidence is not conclusive. You might be wearing a bedsheet for all I can see.

Snickering, I adjusted the bathrobe and extended my arm to take a much broader portrait of myself. It went all the way to my waist, where a loose knot held the robe together. And, as I did this, all the feelings that usually followed a battle on the ice began to stir.

I wished he was here.

Which was an odd feeling. Normally, I would wish to have gone out with Avery. He was going to satiate his hunger just fine. But me? I had no appetite for the random boys and girls of Chicago tonight.

Noah: That could be a doctored photo. I have no way of knowing.

I wrinkled my nose and did something unthinkable. My brain caught up with my thumbs a moment too late and I found myself stuck in the moment of dialing Noah for a video call.

He picked up a moment later, his unruly hair somehow even less tame while he lay in his bed, his shoulders bare because he was, of course, topless. When was he not? I adored that little contradiction about him. He was so awkward and aware of himself at all times, but he so freely shed his clothes when he was alone in his room. It was his safe space, I realized. He could act however he liked when he was enclosed between those four walls.

"Ah, so it really is a bathrobe," he said, his tone flat.

"You sound bitter about it," I pointed out.

"Oh, I preferred imagining you were naked, adding a bathrobe filter," he said. Then, his eyes went wide with fear. "Shit. Are you alone?"

I laughed and shook my head at him. "Avery just went out. I'm all by myself."

Noah shifted so that he now lay on his side and the phone was in his hand, resting on the pillow. The wall with the Christmas lights along the bookshelf was just behind him. "Good. That could have been awkward. I either overthink or don't think at all."

"Mm, that's all great, but let's go back to you imagining me naked. Is that a common phenomenon? Do you go to lectures to learn about particles and fantasize about me?" I teased him, my voice dripping in seductiveness.

Noah turned a shade redder and rolled his eyes, fixing his black-framed glasses with the back of his hand. I'd warned him not to do it like that and it bothered me that I had. He was adorable when he did it so mindlessly. "Actually," he said, a little strangled. "Believe it or not, I don't walk around all day imagining you in all sorts of unholy situations." He bit his lip against a rising smirk, then shook his head. In a low voice, he murmured: "I save that for my evenings."

I laughed, my voice rising by an octave, and my heart stumbled. As if someone pulled at my limbs, I suddenly felt a little more stretched and taut. "And it's evening right now. Ergo..."

"Wow. That is a correct use of 'ergo.' Well done, Sawyer." His eyebrows did a little dance above his eyes.

"I love it when you're a smartass," I husked. "Talk clever to me."

Noah snorted, but it did little to cover up that sensational glow that came over his face when he was getting horny. "Shut up."

"Give me a fun fact, Noah," I pleaded, voice as slutty as I could make it.

He rose to the bait, although his flat expression told me he was well aware of being baited. "Well, in 2004, astronomers discovered a star now known as Lucy. It's a white dwarf. That means it spent its nuclear fuel. Er, stars can either grow so big that they ultimately collapse and turn into black holes or slowly wink out. Lucy's the latter. What's odd about Lucy is that she is essentially a gigantic diamond. Carbon and oxygen in her core crystalized over billions of years, basically forming a diamond that is ten billion trillion trillion carats in size."

I gaped. How the hell did he even have that piece of information inside his head? "Someday, when a guy kneels and offers you a diamond ring, you're gonna be horribly disappointed."

Noah chuckled and I had a feeling he found the idea of someone proposing to him ridiculous, rather than finding my joke humorous. "Right."

We gazed at each other for a short while, silence undisturbed. "Give me another one," I said, making it sound dirty solely with the inflection and tone of my voice.

Noah sighed and obliged. "Did you know our galaxy is being pulled toward a mysterious region of space? We're not alone. Countless other galaxies are moving in that direction. The stars and dust of the Milky Way don't let us see what's there, but we call it the 'Great Attractor.' Nobody knows what it really is. It's a gravitational force we can't explain, but it's pulling us in."

My eyes widened in horror. "What do you think it is?"

He shrugged. "If I knew, I'd have a Nobel Prize by now." He thought about it for a moment, then turned very still and serious. The ominous look he gave me made me think of something apocalyptic. "If I had to guess, I'd say it's a Sawyer-like playboy, who galaxies just can't resist. They're all just falling head over heels."

"Ha-ha. That's so funny. Watch me choke on tears of laughter." I rolled my eyes at being teased so mercilessly, then watched him smirk on my screen.

We talked for a little while longer, then I released him so he could go to sleep. My exam results were still not in and I was slowly going mad over it. The feeling that lived permanently in my heart was of doom and gloom. We'd done so much and I achieved so little. I knew, deep down, that my days were numbered. None of this was going to matter soon enough. I'd be away from the *Titans*, from Noah, from Northwood. Not that one exam would bring on Judgment Day, but it would be the first crack in the poorly constructed wall. And it would all go downhill from there.

But, as I forced myself to eat a little, finding the food tasted like paper napkins compared to the richness all my senses experienced while I'd been on the phone, I understood one thing for certain. I missed Noah.

TEN

Noah

Soon after Sawyer returned from his Chicago trip, I grew to detest most workdays. Our study dates, which were very much about studying and not nearly as much about dating, became a Wednesday evening event, as rare as Halley's comet. But Saturdays were something else entirely.

Each late afternoon, I would find a text message on my screen, requesting — not asking — that I show up at this place or that after my last tutoring session of the day. So was the case for the following four Saturdays, each ending in increasingly more creative lessons behind locked doors. And Sawyer would feather me with kisses each Sunday morning as if he had something to prove. As if there was nothing else he would rather be doing. Then, he would leave, and I would swoon on my own for a while before getting the room ready for the first student's visit.

One such Saturday, when early spring rain trapped us inside my room, Sawyer spun around in my chair like he was five years old and cocked his head to the side. "Why don't you do those competitions anymore?"

"What do you mean?" I asked. It had been a week since we'd last been together, and competitions in physics were the very last thing I wanted to talk about. I had too many other ideas of how to pass the time. Sawyer was wearing a black, short-sleeved T-shirt, sliding down in my chair until the edge of it dragged up and revealed his inked stomach. It was enough to make me drool and more than enough to obliterate all my other thoughts.

"You're tutoring all these students to win the prizes you could take for yourself," Sawyer said.

I shrugged. "It pays well."

He was rubbing his chin in thought, his other hand on the bare stripe of his stomach, feeling his skin. "I'm sure winning would pay better. In the long run."

"I already caught the big fish." My voice gave away nothing, but maybe that in itself gave away plenty. Sawyer narrowed his half-moon eyes at me and shook his head a little. I sighed. "I was fourteen when I won the Olympiad. That's like a child actor becoming famous for their first big screen role. There's no topping it. It just makes the rest of your life...meh."

"Meh?" Sawyer asked, incredulous.

"Meh," I insisted. "Firstly, it gets increasingly harder to win another. Secondly..." I really didn't want to talk about this. I exhaled and rolled my eyes. If only he would take his top off or something. But he watched me intently as if I were talking about the world's most important things. "Mom and Dad decided that because I was *a prodigy*, the Olympiad was now the baseline of success. 'If he can win that at fourteen, he can surely get hired at CERN by eighteen.' Or, 'He could get an honorary degree years earlier.' That sort of bullshit. The pressure was…I dunno, too much. They couldn't understand why I wanted to focus on astrophysics instead of something more practical and experimental. They couldn't understand why I wanted to study on my own terms. They always wanted more, but I couldn't outdo what I'd already done." I shuddered. Bitterness filled me to bursting, and I pulled my knees up to my chin, pressing my back harder against the wall and letting my feet dig into the mattress. "It's like if you won a jackpot and everyone started nagging you to win another jackpot month after month. But you can't. It doesn't work like that. But you can't prove it to them, so you're just permanently a one-trick pony. A single-use wonder. A…a…" I sighed. "A failure."

"Jesus," Sawyer snapped, sliding out of my chair and dropping to my side. He practically grabbed my face and brought his inches away. I could feel his heat on my skin. He ran as hot as ever. "You're not a failure, Noah. You're brilliant. You're the smartest smart-ass I know."

I snorted. "That's…reassuring."

"I mean it. Please don't make me wind you up like a dancing monkey toy. You'll be speaking genius all night if I get my way." He held my face with both hands, staring into my eyes until he saw a flicker of belief in them.

I wasn't sure if I believed him, though. Perhaps I acted it out for his sake. I appreciated his kindness, but I'd spent years considering this carefully. There was a point to what my parents expected of me and why they were disappointed.

It felt like a piece of me died when I won that competition. A little part of my soul lost purpose after that. I hadn't realized it immediately, but I had also built great expectations, just like Mom and Dad. Then, the rest of my life happened, and nothing ever matched the heights I'd reached before I could even shave. *Oh, and you have a full beard to shave now*, I whispered to myself sarcastically.

Sawyer was leaning in as if to prove his point by kissing me. I welcomed it wholeheartedly, but his damn phone dinged just as his lips grazed mine. The sound startled us both. This wasn't a random text message. This was from the university's app.

He began shaking and pulling back, panic threatening to engulf him. "The results. These have to be the results." He pulled his phone out of his pocket as we scrambled off the bed and paced the room. I wanted to tell him something reassuring, but he'd already told me how horribly he'd done. The fact that he couldn't recall any of the questions or answers from the first exam gave me little confidence, but I'd never shown that to him. And I never would, no matter what the results said.

"Oh, shit," Sawyer said, staring at his screen. "They are. The results."

Wallaby was notorious for requesting timely assignments but delivering results at her tortoise pace.

I stared at Sawyer while he moved his trembling thumbs across the screen and gaped. The horror on his face shattered my heart. I had failed him. I had been so occupied with my growing desperation and the need to finally learn how to catch a guy that I hadn't paid enough attention to him.

Damn it. I'd dropped the ball so badly that I wanted to run away and hide.

In his terror, Sawyer dropped his phone. He lifted his shocked gaze to meet my eyes, then took a big step forward, nearly tumbling us both down to the floor. His lips smashed against mine before I knew what was up. Comfort kisses? Was that a thing? If yes, I could do it. I could comfort him. It was the least I could do after failing to help him with his exam.

The intensity of his kiss sent shivers down my spine. It was the most ruthless, lusty kiss I had gotten from him, and he'd been increasingly free with how we made out over the last few weeks.

"Flying colors," he murmured against my lips, and I choked. "Fucking flying colors, you genius."

I grabbed his T-shirt tightly in my fists and pushed his chest away from mine, separating our lips and gaping. "Wh-what do you mean?"

Sawyer blinked fast and shook his head. "I passed. I fucking passed with flying colors. She even gave me extra points for the elaborate responses..." He pulled away, bent down for his phone, then read off his screen. "...and an in-depth understanding of the topics at hand. The concerning lack of effort on the final assignment can be attributed to Professor Jordan's Introduction to Mathematics and overlooked for the purposes of this exam."

"Wait...she...what?" I couldn't figure out how to string words together.

"She gave extra points," Sawyer explained. "So they evened out the difference."

I was still short of understanding, but it didn't matter. I pulled him in and kissed him in return. It was the blazing, violent clash of lips and tongues, careless in its messiness and the embarrassing sounds that came with it.

"Fuck, we need to celebrate," Sawyer said. "Oh hell, Noah, you're a goddamn genius. Thank you *so* much. Let's go out. I wanna dance. I need to dance."

Although he had just presented me with my personal idea of hell, I wasn't going to dampen his moment one bit. Fuck it. We were going dancing. And when he saw my poor attempts at dancing, he would regret ever knowing me, but I would worry about that later.

He grabbed my hand as soon as we had our light jackets on, and we rushed out. "There's this party at the frat house where I spilled vodka all over you. Remember? I think it's appropriate. Right?"

I agreed without considering it. Whatever he wanted, it was his. And Sawyer was practically doing cartwheels and jumping head over heels as we raced through the rain toward the frat house. It was just a couple of buildings away, still in the residential sector of the campus, but we were soaked by the time we barged in.

Sawyer's elated enthusiasm spread so easily to me that I didn't even hate the crowded space at the party. I followed him into the packed room of the large fraternity house where students from all over our campus and beyond congregated.

Sawyer grabbed drinks for us both. "I solemnly swear not to spill vodka all over you," he said, crossing his heart as he lifted his plastic cup of beer.

I shrugged. "But if you do, you'll just have to help me change my clothes."

Sawyer's eyes sparked with desire. Though I'd only made a joke, seeing his interest made my heart ridiculously big.

I wondered if this was what everyone felt like when Sawyer paid them attention. The first time I'd encountered him, in this very house, he was being torn apart by battling twins who wanted a turn. It was like he could cast a spell over you and plant himself in the center of your heart with little more than a mischievous smile or arching of an eyebrow. I found myself pulled into his orbit when he moved a few paces away from me and merged into the sea of dancing people.

Amidst the thumping beats and swirling lights of the frat party, I stood, feeling a bit like a deer who had somehow wandered into a bustling marketplace. But Sawyer had a way of making everything seem like an adventure, even if that adventure involved navigating a sea of red cups and overenthusiastic dancers. I tried my best to keep up, even if my dance moves made me look like I was auditioning for a dad dance competition.

As the music swayed and bodies moved, I couldn't help but feel a gravitational pull toward Sawyer. Our orbits seemed to sync effortlessly, like two stars dancing in the night sky. We kept it low-key, careful not to draw too much attention. I didn't have clear reasons figured out, but it just didn't feel right to throw myself at him. Maybe I knew that guys like Sawyer didn't dance with guys like me. Except, here he was, doing just that. And every time our eyes met, it was like an inside joke only we understood.

Sawyer's laughter rang in my ears as he pulled me deeper into the crowd. "Just move to the rhythm, Noah. No one cares if you're a dancing prodigy or not."

Easy for him to say. I shuffled my feet, a mixture of embarrassment and amusement flooding me. "I'm more of a 'two left feet' kind of guy."

Sawyer's grin was infectious. "Well, your two left feet seem to be getting along just fine with my two right ones."

As minutes passed, our magnetic connection grew stronger, an invisible thread that tugged us closer with every shared smile, every soft touch of our fingers brushing against each other. We danced like no one was watching, even though we were well aware that eyes were on us, curious and intrigued.

"I promise you're the best part of this party," Sawyer murmured, his words creating a bubble of warmth around us.

I chuckled, my heart doing a little pirouette. "And you're the reason I'm not hiding in a corner right now."

We swayed together, but never too close, each step a reminder that this was new territory for me. But with Sawyer so near me, even the unfamiliar had its charms. It was...fucking fantastic. And that pull radiating from Sawyer, bringing all the other celestial objects closer to him, threatened to draw me in despite so many pairs of eyes in the room. I watched him as he bit his lip in ecstatic joy.

I wanted to leap at him and have him right this instant. I wanted to slam my lips against his and take my chance. Maybe, just maybe, we could turn the rules of nature around and see if a Sawyer would go for a Noah of this universe. Out here, in front of everyone. Would he push me away? Would he welcome it? I seriously didn't have a clue. All we'd done was hook up in the privacy of my room, chat in secret, and platonically hang out. Whether real or not, I was sure there was a difference, a barrier, or some invisible threshold that still required crossing.

I counted down from three in my head before leaning into him.

Three.

Two.

What the hell? We both spun simultaneously when something crashed on the other side of the room.

My heart cracked, but the buzz around us was too frantic to let me pay attention to that. On the far side of the room, two guys were rolling on the floor, grappling and attempting to throw punches. The one on top, dark-haired and with an explosive frown on his face, was bleeding from a split eyebrow when I got a glimpse of his face. The other guy wrestled for control and turned them around, but the crowd stepped in and separated the two.

"The fuck? That's Cameron," Sawyer said. "What the hell is going on?"

"Who's Cameron?" I asked in a low voice, trying not to appear thirsty for gossip.

Sawyer pulled me to the side as the crowd began to shift, and the other troublemaker was practically being dragged outside. A few more guys left after him while others shouted for peace. This Cameron person was growling and raising his hands in surrender, escorted by a blond guy that was just as tall and just as handsome as Cameron. "And that's Riley," Sawyer said. "They've been...hell, I don't have a clue what they have been doing. They have this on-again-off-again thing, I think. Fuck, he kicked Jonah's ass." Sawyer shot me a naughty, meddling grin, then gestured for me to follow. We walked through the crowd of upset people, all scoffing and shaking their heads, until we reached the window. Out there, in the pouring rain, Riley and Cameron were visibly agitated.

I couldn't hear a word they were saying, but the jerky, restrained moves of their tight fists told me they were fighting.

"Somebody's in trouble," Sawyer said.

"Do you think we should leave them alone?" I asked, my discomfort at watching a couple fight growing to unbearable levels. Never in my life had I experienced a fight like that. I'd never had a boyfriend to do it with, even if I wanted to. And however awesome it was to learn all these new and wonderful things with Sawyer in my bedroom, I couldn't exactly pretend there was more to it. We weren't really dating.

Just as I took a step back, the unexpected happened. The blond guy, Riley, grabbed the troublemaking Cameron, and the two began to fight. No. They were...kissing.

"What the hell is going on?" Sawyer moaned. "Right. Enough peeping." He laughed, then pulled away from the window. I followed him, but my mind was racing. Out there, those two guys were fighting, kissing, and experiencing a storm of emotions.

And in here, I had no idea where I was heading.

But that didn't matter right now. Sawyer was leading the way, and I could definitely afford to follow him unthinkingly for a while longer.

The truth was, he was way too much fun to be around. Even if the most he ever gave me were these Saturday evenings, I would be happy to have them. It was so much better than what my life had been before.

Cold reason told me it couldn't last, but I silenced my cold reason. The same voice told me I'd failed at everything I'd ever tried after one lucky moment when I was a teen. And that voice could fuck right off tonight because Sawyer had chosen me. No matter what happened next, Sawyer had made me the center of his world tonight.

ELEVEN

Sawyer

THE BLADES OF MY SKATES CUT ACROSS THE ICE as my stick swiped in front of me and the puck ricocheted away from the goalpost.

The cheers erupted through half the rink while the other half groaned and booed. In spite of them, I lifted my stick and pirouetted a little before returning to my post. Whatever these sad little Blizzard Breakers were trying wasn't working this time.

Far ahead, Cameron lifted his gloved fist at me in celebration. He and Riley worked like twins on the offensive, with Caden Jones leading the left wing. Behind him, in visible discord, Beckett Partridge was struggling to align his tactics. Those two were near the top of our team in talent but firmly sitting at the bottom when it came to their performance. Especially now that Cameron and Riley were working for the good of the team. And making out whenever they thought they were alone in the basement of our frat house. I supposed that was as good a way to smooth out the differences as any.

That thought alone made me glance at the front rows

of our supporters. A few familiar faces here and there, a few subtle agents and scouts, and one face that was bored despite the best efforts to conceal it.

I had dragged Noah to this game as my lucky charm. His involvement in my physics test made all the difference, and I wanted to test a hypothesis; Noah's presence made everything better. So far, I had only allowed the Breakers to score three points, one of which I blamed on Beckett glaring at Caden rather than defending the line.

Noah had been reluctant to come. More than that, actually. He outright refused, citing the big crowd and the involvement of sports, two things he could absolutely not stand. It had taken me two weeks to change his mind. In fact, on Wednesday, instead of covering the new grounds in our lessons, I found the surest way of making Noah agree to things that were out of his comfort zone. And now that I possessed this power, I needed to wield it responsibly. Noah had a love-hate relationship with a particular little pleasure technique that put him into an open state of mind. All I had to do was put him into my lap, wrap my left arm around his arms and chest, and use my right hand to bring him as close to the edge of his orgasm as I could, then keep him there until he whimpered and begged and agreed to watch the game. The rewards he received in return were Earth-shattering.

I winked at him, though three other people near him fanned their faces, and Noah rolled his eyes while struggling to keep a smirk off his face.

"If we win," I whispered into his ear before leaving his room on Wednesday. "You're going to be the happiest, luckiest guy in the world afterward." And I meant to keep that promise. Every time we shut the door and pretended the rest of the world didn't exist, pure magic happened.

Noah wasn't even freaking out anymore. He was so ready to let me in and lock the doors, even to hint at things he wanted to do, that I soon started ignoring the rest of the campus. Going out with Avery and the guys was a bit of a challenge lately because they all went to bars with a clear purpose while I sat, sipped my beer, and texted Noah. Oddly, it brought me so much more pleasure to stare at my phone and provoke his snarkiest, rudest replies than to open my playbook and try flirting with someone else. It just felt wrong even to consider it.

Not that we were exclusive or anything. He had his life, and I didn't meddle. I highly doubted he was chasing guys all over campus, but if he was, it was his right. He was just now entering the wild world of college flings, a place I'd existed in for years. It was only natural that he would want to explore all the possibilities.

The thought made me growl to myself despite my best effort to be nonchalant. The truth was, Noah was way too precious to me to tie him down with agreements of exclusivity. I almost wished I'd met him a few years later when he was bored of hooking up and wanting something else.

Something else…

I could almost fit that big, spiky idea inside my skull. Dating. Exclusivity. A relationship.

The crowd erupted into applause and cheers. It pulled me back into the present, and I realized I'd been skating left and right mechanically while my Titans scored another point on the far end of the rink. They snatched the victory while I'd been lost in my thoughts, too far gone to even notice the moment.

Utter chaos spilled through the rink. Half the players on the ice were skating around, bumping into each other in gestures of celebration. Our captain, Riley, threw his helmet away and kissed Cameron shamelessly in front of everyone, to which the enemy captain, Jonah, glowered. His hatred for Cameron was such that he couldn't hide it, but it wasn't a surprise after the two brawled at the party two weeks ago.

Seeing Cameron and Riley grinding and kissing made me wrinkle my nose, but secretly, I was glad they were pushing the boundaries and paving the way for a little more openness on the ice. I'd always been lowkey about my sexuality, never really hiding it but never letting it be the focus. Hell, half my team didn't know I was actually bi. And if they suspected, they didn't snoop around or ask. But here they were, two awesome hockey players, reenacting the opening scenes of a raunchy movie, no less.

There was also a trace of jealousy in me, but it wasn't directed at our captain. I had the strongest urge to skate across the rink and drag Noah out to feel the ice under his shoes, then slam him against the boards and suck the soul out of his mouth. But that would pretty much undo all the work I'd put into keeping this casual and low-pressure for Noah.

The locker room was a frenzy of celebration, a mix of triumphant shouts and the clatter of equipment being tossed around. Victory against the goddamn Breakers was sweet, and the energy in the air was electric. We'd played our hearts out, and it paid off.

Amidst the chaos, Avery slapped me on the back, his gaze as cold and expressionless as a serial killer's, a tiny quirk in one corner of his lips telling me he was as elated as he'd ever been. "We're hitting the bar later to celebrate. Are you coming?"

I had a different plan — one that involved a quieter,

more intimate celebration. My lips curved into a half-smile. "Nah, man, I think I'll pass this time. Got something else in mind."

Avery raised an eyebrow high enough to tell me he was gobsmacked. "Oh? Does it involve going over your physics notes?"

My heart raced just thinking about it. I kept my tone casual. "No."

Avery leaned in, his voice lowered. "Seriously, Sawyer." He sucked his teeth and shook his head a little.

"What? I'm just gonna catch up on some reading. Nothing suspicious about that." I stuffed my dirty uniform into my duffel.

He eyed me skeptically, but I shrugged it off. Just thinking of catching up with Noah tonight while I still rode this high of victory made me dizzy.

Avery clapped me on the shoulder. "Alright. Say 'hi' to your physics notes, and don't do it on my bed."

I snorted, clapping him back. "I absolutely have no idea what you're talking about."

As the team continued their raucous celebration, I slipped away from the locker room, my heart racing with anticipation.

Outside, Noah stood with his tutoring pimp, and I slowed down. He noticed me, then murmured something, and Matt clapped his shoulder before speeding away. A familiar voice reached my ears as I stood there, giving Matt time to leave.

"Hey, Sawyer," she said. It took my eyes a moment to find her. There were several small groups of people scattered around, leaving the rink and making plans for the evenings.

"H-Heather," I blurted. Of all the people I might

have expected, Heather the Brother Slayer was the last on the list. Where was Zach, anyway? "'Sup?"

"'Sup?" She made her way toward me, and I managed a confused glance at Noah before she was in front of me. "What are you doing tonight? You're not with your team."

"I...have plans," I said.

When she arched one eyebrow, she was gorgeous. There was no denying it. But the words she spoke next made me cold all over. "Can you change your plans? I'm free if you can."

I sighed. "That's great. Really. Great. But I'd prefer to keep my plans intact." They involved a truckload of unseemly and unholy activities from now until the first light of a new day. I most definitely wasn't going to change them.

"Are you sure about that?" She made a joke out of it with her light tone. In another set of circumstances, I would have wished I'd scored it with her that first time. Right now, though, it was a huge relief she and Zach had gotten into a fight over me.

"Isn't your brother around?" I asked. "It's weird talking to you without his jealous stare."

She snorted. "He doesn't need to know."

I sighed again, louder. "There's really nothing to know. I...gotta go. See you around." I pushed past her, feeling her seething for a moment or two before she melted out of my consciousness.

Noah stood idly, watching the stars that dotted the night sky as if nobody else was around. The lights of the campus grounds faded the starry sky, and Noah broke his focus when I reached him. He looked at me and shared a lopsided grin. "Everybody wants a piece of you, huh?"

"Not *a* piece, I'm afraid. Everyone wants the same one." The moment those words were out of me, I regretted being so crass, but Noah laughed out loud and wiggled his shoulders.

"Lucky me," he said softly, and the piece everyone wanted stirred until my underwear grew tight. The drive I felt after battling on the ice was through the roof and I wanted to tackle Noah to the ground this instant and then kiss every inch of him. Again, I had to calm myself down and let things go slowly. "Straight to my place?" he asked.

"Uh, actually, we could go to my place," I said. The house was going to be empty for a long time now. And Noah had never been there. We could use a change in surroundings, I figured.

We made our way quietly but quickly across campus, through the student center, and to the other side, where the residential blocks were. Music pounded from the frat house where we'd been two weeks ago and its quality changed as we passed it.

"Fun fact," Noah said, then proceeded to tell me about the sound waves and how they traveled in different directions, so things like music or a speeding motorcycle sounded different when they approached you versus moving away from you. I struggled to keep up, but he boiled it down in his Feynman technique for me like I was a toddler, and I fucking loved it. It made me laugh.

"You should pursue teaching," I said.

Noah snorted. "And stab my dear parents in the back one last time," he said.

My blood curdled. "Do they know you're gay?" My worst fear was that he hid from them because it would be perceived as another stab in the back.

Noah chuckled dryly. "Oh, they know. I gotta give them credit where it's due. They don't care who I'm with. Straight, gay, bi, trans. That's not the condition of their love. Success is."

I struggled to understand that. My dad nearly wept when I told him about the physics exam, and, by right, nobody should have been that happy. Hell, I hadn't been that happy. But that was the way with my parents. Always had been.

Noah needed someone who would look into his eyes and tell him: "You're amazing just the way you are. You're everything I could have wished for and more. The day you change, the stars will go out."

I blinked twice, quickly, and then cleared my throat. "That sucks," I said. It wasn't exactly what I'd hoped to say, but the words that had crossed my mind were suddenly far too large to leave my mouth.

"I'm ruining the good mood," Noah said, then clapped his hands. "Let's stop talking about my parents. I'd much rather see your room."

That tugged on the corners of my lips. It wasn't my room's interior design he wanted to see. I'd already described it to him once before. It's a pretty lifeless place without much charm—nothing like the room he had made his own just a few blocks away.

I marched us into the team house to Noah's pleased sighs. "This is sweet," he said, looking around the ground floor.

"You think?" I asked. "We're never here. Only for breakfast, I think. The real deal is down here." I extended my arm until he put his hand in mine and pulled him gently to follow me. The secret den beneath the house was dotted with arcade games, couches, a large soccer table, a gaming console, bookshelves nobody went near, and a kitchenette with a mini-fridge that packed enough beer to keep a hockey team satiated on a Saturday night.

"Holy shit," Noah blurted.

It made my heart dance when he cursed. It was a small rebellion of his own. Living his life under his parents' scrutiny, he had to vent somehow, and Noah's sailor-like language rounded him in my eyes.

When I shut the basement door and let the silence fall, Noah was still looking around. He made a few steps ahead, his back turned to me and nodded. "This is so cool. Is that the original *Flipper*? Can I?"

I nodded, and Noah grinned, then went to the arcade game against the far wall on the right side of the basement. The orange glow of lamplights and the dim bulbs in the ceiling set the atmosphere just like I wanted it, and I made my way to the fridge to fetch a couple of beers for us. By the time I hooked up the surround system with my phone and found the most recent playlist — one of Noah's Atompunk oddities that made my heart skip and throb — Noah was immersed in the game.

He was so focused on the game that he wasn't even looking around. I knew there were several things in here that Noah couldn't care less about. The soccer table, team flags, old jerseys hanging on the wall, and even the mini-fridge full of beer. But it thrilled me that he found one to his liking.

I leaned against another arcade game, just next to the *Flipper* he was playing, and watched him as he failed to keep the little marble-like ball from falling through the gap at the bottom. The sci-fi noises pinged from the worn-out speaker, and the lights flashed below the protective glass. Noah made frustrated grunts when the *Game Over* sound played.

"You'll get the hang of it," I said. "It takes a bit to get used to it."

"You've played it a lot?" he asked.

I gave him my cockiest smirk and scooted against him. "Watch and learn, kiddo."

He snorted and crossed his arms on his chest. The sweet scent of his cologne lingered in the air where he had just stood, and I lost all focus. He was everything I thought of, though my muscle memory served me well when I began playing. The commands were a little slow to react with the machine's age, but I'd gotten used to it when I first started playing against Sebastian.

I scored double the points Noah had and was still well below the record a mystery legend had set on the machine an unknown number of years ago. "We have this thing going. Whoever beats the record becomes the king of the house that semester. There was no king in the history of the house."

Noah laughed at that. "I guess living with a crowd of people you like has its positive side, too."

I shrugged. "The privacy of the room you get to decorate just how you like isn't all that bad." I looked into his eyes and watched how his lips worked when he spoke next.

"That's true. I wouldn't trade it for anything. But you guys are a team. Believe it or not, I actually watched the game tonight. You're all so...I don't know. Team-like. Like brothers or old-timey comrades. It was really cool." His lips stretched into a smile, and the tip of his tongue crossed them.

"Christ, you're so beautiful," I whispered, leaping

toward him. For a moment, I thought I was about to scare him with such an abrupt move, but he stood still and welcomed me, sliding his arms under mine and wrapping them around my upper back.

Our lips pressed together, and my chest tightened. No. It wasn't exactly like that. It was more like whatever filled my body grew so big that I couldn't contain it. It wanted to burst out of me and keep growing, rising, expanding until it enveloped every trace of us. It was so powerful that it scared me, but I pushed that fear aside and focused on the sweetness of his lips and the warmth of his tongue as it slipped into my mouth.

I clutched his light spring jacket and pushed his tongue back with mine, exploring his mouth like I had countless times before, but I was never bored of trying it again. "You brought us a victory," I said, pulling back just enough to speak. We both moved enough apart so that I could yank his jacket down his arms and then throw my own on the floor. "I knew you would."

"Oh, fuck," he grumbled, pulling me back against his body. "I'll have to come to all your games, now, won't I?"

"Every. Single. One." My grin split my face, and I leaned in, kissing him despite my stretched lips. I kissed him harder as he laughed softly over my lips. God. He really was amazing just the way he was. He really was everything I could wish for. I prayed he would never change. Doubtless, he would outgrow me and his first little fling someday, but that wouldn't dim the joy I felt when I was near him. And it wasn't going to slow me down now.

I touched the small of his back, pushing our bodies tightly. He moaned as my crotch pressed against his, my hard abs rubbing against his flat stomach. As my hands traveled lower, I took a moment to appreciate his sweet, round butt and give it a firm squeeze.

The gesture must have pleased him. He bit my lower lip and growled against my mouth in reply, then kissed me smoothly. He was getting so damn good at this. Not that I minded him clumsily bumping his teeth into mine or overthinking every move he made. I liked him no matter what. I liked his growing confidence as he dragged his hands down the sides of my torso and to my hips. He clutched them, pulling me in, rubbing his front against mine. Despite the denim pants we both wore, there was no mistaking his excitement. He was hard and ready to play. And tonight, I wanted to do things a little differently.

But one step at a time, I reminded myself.

Slowly, gently, I navigated us around so that he leaned against the edge of the pinball machine in standby mode. When he was there, I leaned into him harder, sure he wouldn't topple down under the pressure. Just the proximity to him excited me enough to be hard as all hell, but kissing and touching him, knowing I was the only one who'd ever done it, made him all the more special. He was mine, and nobody else's. There was something magical about knowing that.

He was like a treat everyone else missed out on, unaware he was the sweetest kind.

Mine.

The possessiveness soared through me.

Mine, mine, mine.

To play with.

To take care of.

To pleasure and torment and make happy. Every experience under the sun was new to him, and I could paint a whole damn canvas of them just for him. I could show him everything there was. I could teach him never to be ashamed of himself or his kinks and interests. I could make him fly high and dive low. Ah, so many things I wanted to do to him.

But first, I pulled the hem of his T-shirt over his head. He was so in sync with me that his arms shot up the moment he realized what I was doing, and the T-shirt was gone. His fine, slim torso made my mouth water. His small, light brown nipples were hard, skin prickling around them, and his chest shuddered as he inhaled.

I took my T-shirt off next, then let him take a nice, long look. He never seemed to get bored of that. Sunday mornings, after sleeping naked in his bed all night, he repeatedly dragged his fingertips all over me, feeling me and forcing me into his memory. I knew that was what he was doing. I was doing it, too. Someday, I would think of him, and he would be happy with someone who was more like him and more deserving of his company. And I would be happy for him, but happier still for the memories.

I stepped forward, letting our bodies melt into one another's, welded by the heat we both radiated. A little shiver accompanied each breath he drew, and every contact of my fingertips against his skin made his muscles flinch. I adored how sensitive he was. It made even the slightest little caress feel like a tremendous gesture. He wasn't desensitized to the proximity of another human being. He wasn't so used to the touch of someone's hand that it meant nothing to him. He was so damn innocent and pure. It made me feel purer just to be near him.

Our brows touched. The tip of my nose brushed against his. My stomach pressed against his. "I want to do something to you," I whispered. "I think you're going to like it."

He didn't open his eyes. He didn't even flinch. "Anything."

I kissed him, undoing the button and zipper of his jeans and then letting them slide down his legs. They remained tangled around his knees, but I didn't worry. I would get there soon enough. For now, I kissed him as deeply and intimately as I knew how.

And when his head dropped back, and he let a moan drag out of his body, I descended to my knees. There was so much I wanted to do with him, but time was on our side. Two sophomores living so close to one another, we had plenty of opportunity to explore the heights and the depths of physical pleasures. Right now, I wanted to explore a very specific sort. Right now, I wanted to give him the absolute best I knew how.

On my knees, I pulled his pants down to his ankles and paused while he kicked his shoes off and stepped out of his jeans. His boxer briefs had little carrots printed all over them, and I chuckled. We'd gone through all the fruits and vegetables I could think of. He'd worn eggplants and cucumbers and bananas and zucchinis. Each time I saw him, he wore a new innuendo.

Extending from the middle to his right hip, his hard cock stretched the black fabric thin. Beneath it, bulging, his balls were packed tightly, and the bottom edges of his underwear wrinkled up, revealing the tender skin high on his thighs. He was ticklish there, so I didn't touch him just yet.

Instead, I set my hands on his hips and pulled him in gently. My lips feathered the tip of his cock, and he throbbed against my mouth. Even his breath, as he exhaled, was thin and strained. He was tense all over and grabbed the arcade game's edge with both hands to keep himself grounded.

I placed my left hand on his stomach, and he clasped it with his right, clutching me tightly like letting go would make him drift away. He shivered as I tugged on his underwear, pulling his hard cock down with the waistband until the pressure was such that his soft moans grew louder and morphed into a grunt and a cry. "Fuck," he murmured just as the waistband slipped over the tip of his cock, and his length sprang to full mast.

Noah breathed freely for a moment, his chest rising and expanding, then falling.

I licked my lips while reaching gently between his legs and cupping his balls. Smooth, big, tightening already with the unbearable lust that coursed through his veins as much as mine, I squeezed them just enough to make Noah tense but not uncomfortable. I loved stretching him thin against the sensations I could cause. I loved when he was strung so tightly that every breath of air on his skin made him shudder.

Pressing my left hand harder against his flat, firm stomach, I opened my mouth and took him in, sealing my lips around the head of his cock. His precum's sweet and salty flavor filled my mouth, the scent of soap mixed with fainter traces of his musk. His thin and strained whimper was like the finest melody to me.

I sucked the air out of my mouth and leaned in, impaling my head on his firm and throbbing length. He filled my mouth just perfectly, my right hand open and holding his balls, index and middle fingers reaching further between his legs and feeling his taint. At every little touch and rub, he throbbed. Part of me wanted to torture him until he begged for mercy of release, but the victory had put me in an especially good mood.

I pulled back and shot him a devilish grin, then stuck my two fingers deep into my mouth.

Noah used the opportunity to take himself in his hand and stroke soothingly, but it didn't last. When my index and middle fingers were slick with saliva, I nudged his legs apart. He was beyond words, barely inhaling enough oxygen to keep his brain running. His sweet, smooth face was pink, and beads of sweat gathered on his wrinkled brow. His eyebrows were high above his elegant, black glasses, and his mouth stretched open in an expression of torment and pleasure.

I reached between his legs, fingers slick and warm, and slid the tips between his cheeks. He bit down on his lower lip, cock throbbing freely, leaping and falling, swinging with its own weight.

"Ngh..." He choked and threw his head back as I wrapped my other hand around his thickness, gripping him tightly and feeling every pulse that reacted to my right hand's work. I massaged his rim, savoring the sense of warmth of his body, then added pressure.

He was skilled enough to know what to do. Tension disappeared from his cock and his hole. It melted away as his muscles relaxed to allow me in. And I took the opportunity gladly, burying my index finger inside this sweet, innocent guy.

"Mother...fucker," he cried, his hole clenched enough my knuckle for a moment before he laughed softly with relief. "That was sudden."

His cock throbbed twice in my hand. "You loved it. Don't lie."

"Mm." Instead of searching for words, he put one

hand on my head. He didn't need to push. I was more than willing to please him like this. It mattered to me that Noah would learn and remember that being a top or a bottom didn't dictate any of the dynamics between him and his partner. They were preferred roles but as fluid as I could imagine. Just because I was a top didn't mean I couldn't kneel for him and give him the ride of his life. And just because he was a bottom — or so he had thought when I'd asked — it didn't mean he couldn't grab my head and force me to swallow him whole.

I pressed my second finger against his hole, but I was far gentler this time. Slowly, I added half an inch, stretching him until he moaned and tensed. I pulled back, penetrating him lightly with my index finger, wrapping my lips around the tip of his cock. The flavor of his precum was deliciously stronger.

After a heartbeat or two, I pressed the middle finger against him once more, sliding in with ease. Noah curled his fingers, gripping a fistful of hair on the back of my head, yanking me down on his cock until it pressed against the back of my throat. I was experienced enough — more than enough — in relaxing the muscles in my throat at a moment's notice. He slid in, holding himself deep in me, cutting off the flow of air into my lungs while I buried both fingers deep into him. The longer he held himself lodged in my mouth, the harder I ravaged his tight entrance with slick and skillful fingers.

A cough erupted from me and I jerked my head back, saliva bubbling from the corners of my mouth.

"Fuck, yes," Noah moaned.

He liked it rough and dirty, I noticed. He'd shown me hints of it before, especially when I edged him. The whole truth of it was that Noah liked all shades of it. He could be thrilled with a vanilla missionary quickie as much as with an hour-long torment that left me shivering and begging to come.

As I rammed my fingers into him, quickly leaning down on his hard length, he whimpered and trembled. His other hand gripped the edge of the vintage arcade game almost until it shook.

I sped up, pushing against his special spot and sucking the air out of my mouth to heighten pressure and pleasure both. He whimpered once, crying out a warning in the heartbeat that followed, but I persisted. I wanted to taste him. I wanted to eat him and surprise him when I was fed.

Noah's hole clenched around my knuckles, and he spilled the heat of his pleasure into my mouth. Some trickled down my throat; the rest coated my tongue. Its salty-sweet flavor gave off a hint of pineapple that made my heart trip. He'd read that somewhere and tried it without saying a word. The scent of his sex was like the scent of the first rain after a long drought, refreshing and bringing relief. It filled me to bursting.

Noah throbbed in my mouth rapidly, his hole flexing around my fingers as I gently pulled them out. And, when I felt that he was spent and relaxing, I pulled my head back. After finishing in my mouth, the glazed quality of his eyes excited me beyond belief, and I was twice as determined to surprise him with the extent of my wickedness.

I rose to my feet and looked into his eyes as I licked my lips. Gently, I took him in my hand while he softened, my other hand on the back of his head.

His eyes widened as I leaned in as if I was breaking some sacred rule. He gasped shortly.

"Have you ever tasted yourself?" I whispered.

The blush on his cheeks could have been from the heat of the previous moment, but it could have been from my question, too. He shook his head.

"Do you want to? You're delicious." I let my lips hover over his. My mouth was wet and messy. This moment was sinful enough that I could live the rest of my life as a saint and still be turned away from the Pearly Gates. Oh, I would walk away whistling and with a skip in my stride. If he kissed me now, it would be worth an eternity of damnation.

Noah hesitated only a moment, then smashed his lips against mine, parting them and letting our tongues touch and play. I'd offered him a taste, but he reached and took the whole of it. If I was wicked, he was the Devil himself. I loved it.

He kissed me with the sort of lust a person was near incapable of right after an orgasm. But that was Noah. Insatiable. And he was my perfect match.

TWELVE

Sawyer

THE ANTICIPATION BUBBLED BENEATH MY SKIN like an electric current, making every mundane action feel charged with inexplicable excitement. As I stood under the warm cascade of the shower, I couldn't help but grin like a fool, the water masking the goofy smile that had taken up residence on my face. It had been a week — a painfully long week — since Noah and I had spent the entire night together. We'd done little talking and a great deal of kissing practice. I'd pleasured him in the basement, then moved us to my room. And when I sensed Avery and the guys might be thinking of returning, we'd strolled back to Noah's place for the rest of the night. We hadn't closed our eyes all night long, but the week that followed had been a grind. The *Titans* had a guest match in Pittsburgh, and life had gotten too busy for Noah. But tonight was different.

I turned off the shower, my fingers lingering on the tiles as I let out a contented sigh. My mind raced with thoughts of Noah, of the way his eyes sparkled when he laughed and the way his shy smile could melt even the toughest of defenses. It was just for fun, I reminded myself. Just two guys hooking up. For practice. But the fluttery feeling in my stomach told me it was more than that.

With a towel wrapped around my waist, I padded into the room where Avery sprawled out on his bed. I glanced at the clock. It was still early evening, but every minute that separated me from seeing Noah felt like an eternity. I chose a decent outfit — a pair of black jeans matched with a black henley and a hoodie I would put on later to keep me warm on his roof — and went to the kitchen. I rustled up something simple to eat—a grilled cheese, something that wouldn't ruin any romantic plans I might have swirling in my head.

After a quick bite, I faced the bathroom mirror, toothbrush in hand. As I brushed my teeth, I couldn't shake the image of Noah's smile from my mind. God, was I this gone? This smitten? It was just a regular night. But it wasn't. Usually, we would catch up and then dive into the thrills we had both been anticipating for days, but tonight was the night of the meteor shower. I wondered if he knew. He probably did, but he had never mentioned it. And I hadn't said a word either. Instead, I prepared a playlist on my phone and a bottle of wine, planning to take him to the roof of his dormitory, far enough above the campus lights to give us a clear view of the northern sky and the shooting stars.

I was giddy just imagining his expression.

"You're pacing," Avery pointed out.

I snorted. "I'm not pacing."

Avery cleared his throat. "You are walking in a straight line from the door to the desk and back. You are literally pacing."

"Fine. I'm pacing." I spread my arms in surrender and shrugged in challenge. "So?"

"So, why?" Avery asked. He set his phone on the nightstand and focused his gray eyes on me. "What's the matter?"

"Nothing," I said flatly. And nothing was. I didn't have a reason for the tingling in my fingertips and the restless curling of my toes. I didn't have a reason to feel like I'd swallowed a steel blade that was slashing through my insides. It was just some grilled cheese, for fuck's sake. But here I was, feeling like the ground would open up and swallow me whole. Feeling like my skin was too tight for me.

But I couldn't handle this waiting, as if something was about to happen. The sense of foreboding filled me. It was the unbearable feeling that I was at a breaking point. Breaking point of what? I had no idea. But something was happening.

The weeks of casual fun had cost me something big, but I wasn't able to clearly put my finger on it. It irked me that I was nervous. The only difference in what I planned tonight versus any other meet-up was that I didn't just want to hook up. Not that I was bored. Hell no. But I wanted to sit with him and gaze up at the sky and listen to him talk.

And I knew how risky that whole thing was.

I checked the time, though the window already told me I should be going soon. It was getting dark outside. "I should leave," I said, agitated before I could stop myself. Why was he so interested, anyway?

Avery sat up, set his feet on the floor, and looked into my eyes. "I'm sure he's dying to spend time with you when you're on edge like this."

"Is that...sarcasm?" I asked, incredulous.

Avery blinked. "You're evading."

I sighed and growled at the same time, then plopped into my chair and stared at my best friend and current greatest annoyance. "Fine. But don't tell anyone. I've, uh..." I bit my lip and considered my words. "I've been seeing someone."

Silence followed my statement.

Avery didn't flinch. "You don't say."

I scoffed. "But it's complicated."

"You are a mystery that keeps unraveling," he said, looking into my eyes coolly.

"And *you* are getting cocky. Just because some chick taught you sarcasm, you don't have to rub my nose in it." I narrowed my eyes at him. To be honest, it suited him. I just wished I could be as composed as he was. "Anyway, he...I guess, first of all, he's a he. But it's...not so simple. I don't know how to explain it..." *Without giving Noah's personal things away. I'm not outing him as a virgin before meeting me.*

"Let me try," Avery said. "You met this guy. Let's just call him — oh, I don't know — Professor Physics. And Professor Physics got under your skin. And you're scared about what that will do to your reputation."

I couldn't believe several things he had just said, but mainly how wrong he got it. It wasn't my reputation I was worried about. If anything, being around Noah cleared my reputation up some. I shook my head. "First of all, I don't even know how you came up with that pseudonym."

Avery exhaled shortly through his nose, basically rapturing with laughter in normal people's terms. "Let's just say you haven't bitched about studying all semester."

"Ah, so you noticed that," I said, then pushed that can of worms aside and focused on the timely problem. "I don't know what to do. And I need you to swear you won't speak a word of this to anyone."

Avery crossed his heart. Footsteps thudded on the stairs and hallway outside the room.

"I feel like we've been sneaking around for too long," I admitted. "It's for his own good. He's, uh..." Damn. There was no subtle way of putting it, but I tried. "He's not like us, Avery. He doesn't screw around."

"I don't understand," Avery said. "You want a boyfriend who screws around?"

I pinched the bridge of my nose. "No. I don't want him to be my boyfriend." *Because that will just get him stuck with his first guy, and he'll miss out on all the things I had plenty of.* "He's too inexperienced for a relationship," I said, agitation rising. "It's too soon. He's definitely not ready for something like that. Hell, I don't even know if I'm ready. Or if I'll ever be."

Avery sucked his teeth. "That's a tough one."

I glared at him. "'That's a tough one?' Is that all you have to say after dragging it out of me?" I wanted to sit with Noah and gaze at the night sky and make wishes. I wanted the sweet, relaxed evenings in the company of a guy who made my heart dance like mad. I wanted...ah, I wanted what was best for Noah. And tangling him into the confines of a relationship wasn't right.

"I'm thinking," Avery said. He blinked once, then nodded. "You need to tell him."

And pressure him into wasting the years meant for exploration on me? "Out of the question."

"I don't see another way," Avery said.

I shrugged. I really wanted to just sit with Noah and

take his hand in mine. But maybe that was the whole problem. I was putting my wishes first instead of considering what he needed now. Holding his hand would suit me just fine. I was tired of chasing cheap thrills. But Noah hadn't even had a taste of it.

So, instead of being selfish and luring him into a trap that would only result in resentment, I had to do the right thing. No matter how much it hurt my heart to recognize it, I knew I was the problem. I'd done too much, too often, to be any good for him. He needed to go out there and make mistakes, fall in love, get his heart broken, sleep around, then find the same conclusion I did. I only wished I'd met him a couple of years later when he was sick of this lifestyle as much as I was of mine.

I inhaled and held that breath of air in my lungs then sighed. "I see another way."

Footsteps thudded abruptly on the other side of the door, and a frown creased my brow.

Noah

There was a meteor shower tonight, and I had the best idea ever.

I'd already played it out in my head a million times. This was the right moment. We were in the middle of the semester and we knew that two more years still lay ahead of us. That was plenty of time to figure stuff out. But I'd already figured out the most important.

When I saw him skating across the ice last week, my heart stumbled repeatedly. When I saw him caught by Heather afterward, jealousy filled me so much that I only knew the red heat of rage. He was mine, I had thought to myself.

And it all made perfect sense. But one piece was missing. I needed to tell him. I needed to tell him and hope for the best.

When I realized the meteor shower was happening tonight, when we normally spent time together, everything fell into place. I imagined it so clearly, even now, as I walked across campus from my place to his to surprise him and make sure he was with me on time.

"There it is," I would say and point at the sky.

Sawyer would look up, and his eyes would sparkle the same way they did when he was following a puck on the ice. "Make a wish," he'd say.

I would. I had my wish on the tip of my tongue. "Done."

"What did you wish for?" he would ask, of course, and I would protest. We would bicker about it until he saw a shooting star, too.

My fantasies split there into a million different ones. He made a wish on one and we decided to reveal them to each other. In another, Sawyer looked at me flatly and said: "I made my wish. I wished for you to tell me what you wished for."

And I laughed and told him.

Because I couldn't keep him otherwise. Heathers and Zachs gathered around him like he was glazed with honey. But I was the one who would do the licking. It had to be me, and I didn't care what anyone else thought.

Or, at least, I had to try.

The team house was quiet when I knocked on the door.

"Yeah?" A lazy drawl came from the other side.

I figured that was invitation enough. I was ecstatic, but I covered it up with a straight-ish tone and a bro-like nod when I entered the house. The guy at the kitchen island looked familiar from the ice. Partridge, I was sure.

"Hey," I said, no longer passing for straight. What the hell was that instinct to hide from straight guys? To draw as little attention as possible, I guessed. I sighed to myself, then licked my lips. "I'm Sawyer's friend. Is he around?"

"Yeah, I think I saw you with him," the tall, floppy-haired guy said. He looked like there was a permanent pout on his lips, though his eyes were self-satisfied, like he knew my deepest, darkest secrets and how to use them against me. I wasn't sure I liked him. "You're his tutor."

"Right," I said. *Not for much longer, I hope*, I thought. If my wish came true, I would be a little more than that. I hoped to seal it with a kiss under the starry sky and stop hiding. I hoped to be more than his physics tutor or his dating pupil. I wanted the whole thing if he would give it to me. And the only way to know for sure was to toss the dice and hope for the best.

"He's in his room. I saw him go in." Partridge pointed to the top of the staircase.

I thanked him, then headed up. It was only when I reached the middle of the staircase that I remembered I should have asked which room was his. I knew, but now this guy knew that I knew.

This is why I hate sneaking around, I thought. It was too late to turn and ask now, so I went up and to the right, approaching the end of the hallway.

I lifted my fist to knock on Sawyer's door but paused when I heard voices.

The muffled voice belonged to Sawyer, and he was audibly agitated. "...his own good. He's, uh... He's not like us, Avery. He doesn't screw around."

"I don't understand," the other guy, Avery, said. "You want a boyfriend who screws around?"

I should have turned away then. I knew I should have. And it shamed me that I stood still. They were talking about me. I couldn't discern what they were truly saying, but Avery mentioned a boyfriend. That word... It nearly tugged on the corners of my lips until I heard Sawyer snap again.

"No. I don't want him to be my boyfriend. He's too inexperienced for a relationship," he said, and I felt a pit open in my stomach. "It's too soon. He's definitely not ready for something like that. Hell, I don't even know if I'm ready. Or if I'll ever be."

"That's a tough one."

My ears rang, and my face heated up. I wasn't supposed to be hearing this.

And he wasn't supposed to be saying it, either.

It wasn't fair.

"'That's a tough one?' Is that all you have to say after dragging it out of me?"

"I'm thinking," Avery said. "You need to tell him."

"Out of the question." The determined tone of his voice fractured whatever was left intact in my chest. Surely, my heart was in smithereens.

"I don't see another way," Avery said.

"I see another way."

The ringing drowned out whatever else he might have said. I spun away as fast as I could, trembling and wanting to scream. I descended the stairs as much as I tumbled down them, not caring whether I tripped and fell or knocked that intimidatingly straight guy off his feet.

I raced across the ground floor.

"Wh-what happened?" Partridge — or whatever the hell his name was — asked.

I heard movement far behind me, doors opening, but I was already leaving, and I shut the door after me. It was only after I had left the front yard and made my way swiftly toward the dormitory that I let myself breathe.

A shudder thundered out of me. This was why I'd been holding my breath. I couldn't trust myself to make a sound without collapsing. I covered my face and paused, letting the trembling wave pass through me, then balled my fists and straightened my arms by my sides.

What the hell had I been expecting? That someone like Sawyer would want to be serious with me? As if! I had nothing to offer but overblown dreams that had no basis in reality. He was one of the most popular guys on campus. And I had been a virgin until he'd pitied me enough to help me be rid of it.

I stormed the dormitory and marched ahead. The bitterness that covered my tastebuds was of my own making. How could I have let this happen? I was smarter than this. I should have known there would be no future here.

I gritted my teeth and decided against shutting myself off in my room.

Perhaps tonight, I could wish to erase the last few months from my memory. And if there were any justice in this cold, dying universe, that wish would come true.

Sawyer

"Shit," I said, looking at Avery, horrified. As I leaped for the door, my heart was racing. Refusing to recognize what I already knew, deep down, I pulled the door open and felt my heart drop into my stomach.

Noah's floppy, light brown curls were unmistakable when I spotted him racing for the main door. By the time I managed to open my mouth to call after him, the door swung open and then shut.

"What the hell was that?" Beckett asked from the kitchen island, where he was scraping off the burnt side of a piece of toast.

I had no time to explain. I only turned to Avery with a look that was devoid of emotion. I tried to go over all the things I'd said. I'd outed him as inexperienced to a total stranger — no matter that Avery was my best friend; I had no right — and I had…oh shit! I had declared there could never be anything between us.

Fuck. My. Life.

"Go," Avery said, urgency touching his usually cool voice. It must be important if Avery was showing emotion. "Fucking go after him," he snapped impatiently.

I nodded, my throat choking up.

"And tell him how you feel, dammit," Avery said when I hadn't moved. "Don't go around it, Sawyer. Just tell him."

"Yeah. Okay. Right." I murmured these words one

after another, my mind spinning. I had to. I couldn't avoid it.

My feet finally moved. I found myself hurrying out of the room without even a jacket. I walked into the cool spring air, but my body radiated heat of shock and urgency that even a hoodie seemed too much.

I ran out and down the paved path connecting our house with the rest of the campus.

My heart was skipping every other beat. What the hell had I done? He'd run away so quickly that I could only imagine he'd heard the worst in everything I'd said.

I knew I had to set him free, but not like this. I hadn't meant for him to overhear it. I had only ever wanted to make everything better for him, not to break his heart.

What have I done? What have I fucking done? The words spun around my mind as I reached the dormitory and barged in, then ran up the stairs toward his room. The last time I came here, we had been high on lust and tumbling up the stairs while making out and touching each other's bodies all over the place. We had indulged in such pleasures that this world had never known. We had given our bodies to one another for the entire night.

If only it never had to end.

I knocked on his door nervously. I didn't know what to tell him or what I would find. If he hated me for this, I couldn't blame him. But it would hurt more than I could bear.

Nothing. Silence met me even when I knocked again.

I reached for the doorknob, my heart thundering in my chest as I turned it.

Locked.

Where the hell was he?

What had I done?

But then, in an instant of blinding realization, it made sense. Of course, Noah knew tonight was the meteor shower night. If anyone would know that, it was him.

I glanced at the other end of the hallway, where a door hung open, showing me the staircase to the rooftop terrace. There was no other place he could be; I was sure of that. I inhaled and held my breath, then moved slowly to the door. The short staircase was narrow and bare, opening up at the top to the starry sky and a few square feet of tranquil space in an otherwise bustling campus. And up there, as I walked out, facing away from me, was Noah Foster.

My heart clenched at the first sight of him.

Far beyond the outline of his unruly hair, blazing across the night sky, a shooting star sparked to life and winked out in a heartbeat. This wasn't how I'd imagined this night would go.

"Noah?" I called, stepping closer.

He was still for a while longer, looking up at the starry sky. The silence extended until the distant traffic seemed to be roaring in my ears. Some party or another on the block had music that flooded the night. Even crickets in the scattered green spaces on campus seemed to be working extra hard in the moments of Noah's silence. I began believing he either hadn't heard or wouldn't reply. But then, he spoke at last. And the words that left his lips were the last I expected to hear. "I shouldn't have eavesdropped. I'm sorry."

I quickly took two paces closer. "What? No. Don't be sorry for that." I wanted to clear the air and explain what I'd meant, but I also didn't want to push him any way he didn't want to go.

Noah shrugged, his shoulders poking up. He turned slowly on his heels, and I got a good look at his disappointed expression.

"I didn't mean..." I meant to say.

"It's okay," he interrupted.

"It's really not," I insisted. "Not like that."

"What difference does it make?" he asked. "Overhearing it through the door or hearing you say it to my face. It's the same thing in the end."

I sighed, but my throat was tightening. The difference was that I wanted to set him free, not break him into pieces and shatter his confidence.

"Seriously, I get it." But his eyes caught the distant lights of campus and the city beyond it, shimmering brighter than dry eyes could. Tears, I realized. And my heart fractured. Noah inhaled, but it was shallow and strained. "You're Sawyer Price — the star keeper everyone wants to be with. You're like that celestial object that draws all the worlds nearer. Is it any surprise I got pulled into your orbit?" He licked his lips and shook his head as if to dismiss his own foolishness. But he wasn't foolish at all. Not to me. "And I know I'll never be good enough, or hot enough, or popular enough for a guy like you." It was a strangled whisper, his choking throat letting him say nothing more.

Tears welled in my eyes, stinging, blurring the whole world before me. But I could make him out. I could make out those green eyes and the hurt and wonder battling in them.

What a goddamn mess we made. What a ridiculous mistake it was. All this time, keeping him at arm's length for his own good...I was a fool. A damn fool. Who the hell was I to decide what was good for Noah? In doing it, I'd nearly changed the perfection that he was.

I set my hands on his face. He didn't flinch. The welling sob in my chest very nearly rose to my throat. But I swallowed and licked my lips, then blinked the tears away. They seared my cheeks on their way down. Quietly, I told him the only thing I knew was true. "You are amazing just the way you are. You are everything I could have wished for and more." My throat seized, and I drew a shallow breath to relax it. "The day you change, the stars will go out."

For a moment, I could see a different timeline. There, Noah pulled away from me and did exactly what I'd always expected him to do. He embraced the lonely player lifestyle, acting out his fantasies with a score of guys who would undoubtedly want him. But that wasn't Noah at all. Not my Noah.

"I didn't want to steal your thrills," I admitted, my voice cracking. "I'm so stupid, Noah, but you know that already. I thought I was setting you free. Why would a smart guy like you want to miss out on all the cheap fun for the sake of being with me?" But I had never looked at things through his eyes.

"You are my thrills," Noah said in a small voice, confirming just how blindingly dumb I had been. "I know I'm no good at this, Sawyer, but I thought we had something..." He let it linger in the air.

And I finished. "...special."

He nodded. Tears spilled down his cheeks as he lifted a hopeful look at me. I brushed his tears away.

"We do," I whispered. "I promise, it's special. I've never had this with anyone. And you...hell, Noah, you need to stop having such a low opinion of yourself. You're the most exciting partner I've ever been with."

A chuckle that was equal parts a sob broke out of him. "I hardly believe that, but thanks."

"I mean it," I said, clutching his face tighter. "Across the board, boys and girls, they were all just fun. But you… you make me feel alive. You make me think there's so much more to life than just hooking up. And that's something I never felt before." I leaned a few inches closer, looking into his eyes intently until he believed me. "I promise, I'll never again just assume how you feel. It was stupid to think that. But I honestly thought it was selfish to tie you to myself just because you make me feel better than anyone ever did."

Noah pulled his lower lip between his teeth and watched me for a heartbeat or two. "But you make me feel that way, too. And call me selfish, but I want to, literally, tie you to myself."

I laughed at that, but the nervousness that rocked me made my laughter shaky. "I'm down for all kinds of things."

"That's…one of the things I…" Breath hitched in his throat, and he blinked rapidly, then lifted his chin a little higher. "…one of the things I…love about you."

My heart hammered so fast and so abruptly that I nearly stumbled. I tried to chase thoughts that swirled through my head, but they were too erratic and random and quick for me to keep up.

"It's not just that, though," Noah said. "You're kind and caring even though you pretend you're tough and bored. But I guess that flirting tactic does work because I fell hard for you, Sawyer. You're funny and confident even when you're wrong and so much smarter than you think. And I...I love you."

I realized then that I was trembling. I really hoped this wasn't a dream or a glitch if Noah's simulation theory was correct. I wanted it to be real, but I wasn't going to pinch myself and accidentally wake up in case I was dreaming.

Instead, I licked my lips nervously and fought against blinking. Every fraction of the second my eyes were closed was a fraction of a second I wouldn't see his beautiful face and his shimmering eyes. What a waste that would be. "You're the best guy I ever met," I said. "I love your weird music. I love your endless tangents about space. I love how you tolerate my Uranus and black hole jokes. And since the first lesson you gave me, I loved everything you cared about. And if that isn't love, I don't know what is. I'm...I'm...I'm so in love with you, you can't even imagine." The words spilled out of me, and each one made his eyes brighter and his smile broader. He was fighting that splitting grin hard by the end. And then, I made him lose the battle against it. "I love you, Noah."

The corners of his lips stretched so wide, and his eyes glimmered so much that I laughed. My heart danced, and laughter erupted from me loudly as I heard the words I'd just said. Every last one was true. And they hardly did justice to the true extent of my feelings.

But where words couldn't do it justice, lips still had a chance.

"Can I kiss you?" I asked.

Noah laughed, blinking new tears away. "I love that you think you have to ask."

I leaned in, closing the small distance between us, and pressed my lips against his. The first kiss was soft but so intense and passionate that all the ruthless, lust-filled kisses of our past paled in comparison. I kissed him for a long time, inhaling through my nose and letting the sweet scent of his cologne sink deep into my memory. It ticked every good feeling I had ever experienced. It brought to life every joy, small and big, from all the times I had seen Noah and all the years before I had even met him. Every happy Christmas morning and every cheer of the crowds that watched me on the ice. His scent and his flavor brought all of it together.

I kissed him while the sky lit up with shooting stars. And when we parted and looked up at the blazing meteor trails, I still held him close. Countless fiery tails of shooting stars winked into life, but I had no more wishes needing to come true. I had a brilliant, loving guy in my arms, and he was so much more than I could wish for.

Epilogue

SIX MONTHS LATER

SAWYER DIDN'T SEE ME RIGHT AWAY. HE WAS busy looking at the row of trees along the lane and their flaming red and orange leaves. They caught the lamplights, which made them even more fiery. Heaps of dead leaves were scattered across the lawns all around campus as the entire hemisphere prepared for a long sleep. Pumpkin spice and hot chocolate became a daily treat, and mist and rain kept us inside, which was always the best way to spend time with Sawyer.

While my schedule was packed with tutoring commitments, Sawyer was hard-pressed to prove himself on the ice. He never missed his practice or conditioning and he rarely missed the social events that kept the team close-knit. He reveled in the glory each game brought him, and while I attended some of his games when they were in the city, I mostly came along to those social events. His team had changed this fall when Riley and Cameron had left and a new generation of athletes arrived. The discord over the captaincy and new rivalries left Sawyer torn, and new loyalties replaced the old.

But he never missed a date. Even now, when a whole week had passed — a rarity, these days, as we spent more time together with every passing month — he was coming.

He spotted me sitting on a bench in a pool of orange lamplight. His face lit up, and he pulled earbuds from his ears, tucking them into the small charging box and then into his pocket. He crossed the distance with a grin on his face, then plopped down next to me, wrapping his arms around my torso and squeezing all the air out of me. "Fuck, I missed you."

I gasped and managed to reply, "I missed you, too."

He groaned and spoke into the nape of my neck. "It was horrible. I don't wanna talk about it. All four days, those two nut-heads were on the verge of murdering each other. They cost us the game in the end."

I exhaled in disappointment. I didn't care who won or lost so much as I cared how Sawyer felt. And when it mattered to him, it mattered to me. "I thought Caden would be above that."

Sawyer pulled back and laughed bitterly. "Oh, Caden is very clearly and loudly above all that. That's half the problem. He's so above it that Beckett sees it as a challenge. And I half believe Coach Murray is doing this to stir the pot."

I scratched the back of Sawyer's neck. His head dropped back and he nearly purred. "Where does all that leave you?" I asked.

He sniffed. "In an awkward corner of hell, my love. I see Caden's point, but he's going about it in all the wrong ways. It's like he's boycotting hockey. He's going around to bars, hooking up, coming late to practice, doing his own thing on the ice. It's really fucking hard to support him when he's like that."

"Haven't you asked him why?" I shook my head in disbelief. I knew there was tension, but I hadn't realized just how much.

Sawyer rolled his eyes. "He said, 'And what did playing by the rules get me?' And honestly, I couldn't even argue with that logic. It wasn't fair, but this isn't a solution either."

I rested my other hand on his cheek and turned his head to look into his dazzling half-moon eyes. The worry melted away from them, and his pupils dilated. My heart skipped a beat. He was so beautiful with his black hoodie and the big duffel hanging on his back. He'd returned from the away game this morning, but I'd had a full day booked for tutoring. And when my schedule freed, he had practice. But I had him now. And Sawyer was always the sexiest after training. Something about him glowed like there was an actual fire in him.

He blinked, then folded his lips briefly. "Let's leave all that behind," he said. "I hate that I've barely seen you this whole week."

I let my hands slide down to his arms, then found his hand on my lap and covered it with mine. "I hate it, too, but it's not gonna be like this forever."

"That's what I've been thinking," Sawyer said. He moved his hand around, and suddenly, our places swapped, his hand over mine. He wrapped his fingers around mine, then stood up and pulled me after him. I followed gladly, and we headed down the lane toward the dormitory. "The thing is, my hockey scholarship covers accommodation, enough to get a room. Yours does, too.

Two rooms make an apartment, right? So, I figured we might want to look at some options if you think that's smart. Maybe I'm missing some huge red flag, but any way I look at it, I discover that a one-bedroom apartment makes the most sense. Can you imagine?" He kept shrugging like it was no big deal as we reached the main door to the dormitory and walked in.

My heart leaped. Not only could I imagine it, but I could sign up to live it this very instant. We climbed the stairs as images poured into my mind. "Living together? That's...fucking brilliant."

"You think?" He was genuinely surprised I agreed. A grin split his face as I unlocked the door to my room. It had gotten too small and confining when it was the two of us in there.

"Hell yeah," I huffed, shutting the door behind us. "I didn't think you would want to leave the team house."

"It's just the house," Sawyer said. "I'm not abandoning my friends, right? Besides, I found three candidates just off campus."

I blinked at him in even greater shock. "You were looking?"

His smile turned from bright to shy in an instant. He threw one hand behind his back and began scratching awkwardly. His biceps bulged in his well-fitted hoodie. "Yeah, I...figured, you know, I might as well see what the price range is. On the bright side, you have more students than ever, and my folks are turning things around. They'll be able to help out. And I'll get representation this year; I can feel it. It's not even a pipe dream. Riley and Cameron's agent was in Indianapolis for the game."

I stopped him there with an abrupt, desperate kiss on his lips. His words ceased and he leaned into the kiss fully.

He was starting to ramble as if I needed any convincing. In the back of my head, my brain still chugged on, and I assessed the situation coldly and reasonably. It was risky. There was no promise of success. Representation for Sawyer would be huge and he would inevitably get it eventually. It didn't change anything now, though, but it didn't need to. I was talking to several other students, one in animation and another in video production, about forming crash courses and scaling up my tutoring gig. I could do more good if I moved from a one-on-one model to something more advanced.

But none of that mattered now. His lips were on mine, and his words were a distant echo in my mind. I kissed him harder, thrusting my tongue between his lips and meeting the tip of his. He welcomed it eagerly, opening his mouth and pushing his tongue back at me. Heat radiated from his body like there was a fire burning in his pants. There probably was, the metaphorical kind, and I was more than happy to reach down and check.

At the first brush of my hand, he throbbed hard. It really had been a week since the last night we'd spent together. We'd had drinks once since then, but I craved his body against mine in a way we could only do in the privacy of my room. Or our shared place in the foreseeable future.

Though I tried to turn us around, Sawyer was far stronger. He spun and pinned me against the door with a thump, making me gasp. It was my favorite spot in the world, between Sawyer and a hard place.

Sawyer moved his lips away from mine, letting me breathe in through my mouth, and kissed the length of my neck. His left hand rose to the back of my head, and he ran his fingers through my unruly hair. His kisses were fierce and ruthless, and his murmurs were strained and tight-voice. "Love you so fucking much," he said over and over as if holding back the urge to shout it from the top of his lungs.

It was a familiar feeling. Whenever he was near me, I wanted to sing those words in the most rapturous tone I could pull off. I loved him. I wanted everyone to know it.

Aside from wanting to brag to everyone I met that Sawyer Price was my boyfriend, I wanted to feel his body against mine. Just like this.

He thrust his hips, his crotch pressing against mine, and a flutter rose from my stomach. Heat uncoiled in me, and I swiped my hand between us, feeling his hard length inside his pants. He made a choked sound in his throat, and I knew, once and for all, just how happy he was to see me.

Grinding against me, Sawyer sealed his lips on my neck and sucked until I wiggled free of him, preventing an embarrassing hickey from marking me for a week.

Sawyer chuckled, then pulled back. "You don't mind that I was searching for a place?" he asked, his lips stretching a little to form a gentle smile.

"Do I look like I mind?" I asked. I was aware of my heated face and glazed eyes. I was aware that every detail spoke of the indestructible lust that could only be quenched one way. And I was visibly determined to have it. "I love that you did that," I admitted.

Sawyer snatched my wrists before I knew what was happening, lifting my arms high above my head and thunking my hands against the top of the door, trapping me in one swipe of his hand that clutched both my wrists. His other hand traveled to my waist, where my hoodie had lifted to reveal an inch of my skin. He slipped his hand under my hoodie and felt the side of my torso all the way from my hip, over my ribcage, and to my armpit. I thrashed in an attempt to free myself, tickled by his fingertips on my armpit, but Sawyer had such a powerful grip on me that I couldn't break out of it.

He was also merciful enough to stop tickling me. Instead, his hand moved under my hoodie to the side of my left pec, following the curved line that attested to somewhat of a serious workout regiment I had introduced into my life. He was very pleased about that, kissing me harder until his fingers found my nipple and pinched it so hard that I yelped. Shivers ran down to my groin, making my cock throb painfully, and my hips thrust forward to clash with Sawyer's. My crotch rubbed against his, and I whimpered over his lips.

"You're so horny," Sawyer pointed out in his voice of absolute pleasure and pride. He was cocky, and I loved him just like that.

"A week is too long," I whispered, my whole body too tense for conversation.

Sawyer's eyes sparked with mischief. He pulled back from me, released my arms, and then did precisely what I needed him to do to me. I wouldn't have been able to ask him so exactly to do this had he given me the chance.

Sawyer grabbed my hips and spun me around, pinning my front to the door and leaning against my back. His erection, trapped in his pants, pressed hard against my butt. I could feel the pulse of excitement course through him.

Sawyer leaned on me with all he had, squeezing me tightly against the door and moving his whole body in a dance-like flow. His chest pressed against my upper back, his crotch on my ass, his legs firmly set between mine, feet shuffling further out to spread my legs even more. His hands ran from my shoulders to my wrists and back, then over the middle of my torso and down, down, down. When he reached my groin, he hooked his hands there. The immense pressure turned unbearable when Sawyer tugged me gently up, lifting me to the tips of my toes and further. For a skinny guy who played up his nimbleness and swiftness as his greatest strengths, Sawyer could lift me with surprising ease.

I bit down on my lower lip to stop the moans from dragging out of me. The door between me and the rest of the world was simple wood. It would let sounds travel if anyone passed down the hallway.

The strain of having my feet hang while Sawyer kissed my neck from behind built up the pressure in my chest. I held my breath and cried for pleasure until he let me fall back to my feet. Then, a grunt escaped me, and I thrust my butt back against his crotch.

Sawyer's hands moved quickly around my waist, cupping my cheeks and squeezing firmly. He moved his hands around, circling and massaging, appreciating me for all I was. Then, in a swift move, his hands dragged back up and around to feel my flat stomach and rose higher. He dragged my hoodie up and up and up until he was holding my chest and reaching for my neck, folds of fabric slowing him down.

I pushed myself back from the door, threw the hoodie up over my head, let it fall on the floor, and leaned against the door again. Sawyer explored me as if this was our first time, feeling every inch of me. He kissed the back of my neck, my shoulders, the length of my spine. Each contact of his lips on my skin sent shivers in every direction. And the lower he moved, the more tense I became until it felt like I was on the verge of tears with the sheer sensitivity of my body. Every cell in me was alight. Every part of me was eager to feel his lips.

Sawyer lowered himself to his knees, kissing the small of my back with wet lips, letting the tip of his tongue reach out and meet my body here and there, and running his hands along the sides of my torso.

When his lips brushed against the edge of my denim pants, Sawyer moved his nimble fingers to the button in front, undid it, and pulled the zipper down. I was, by now, gone too far for words. A grunt of approval left my throat as he yanked my pants down my legs, leaving them tangled around my knees.

His right hand swiped over the bulge in my lucky, cucumber-covered underwear, lightly tickling the sensitive tip until I coiled and pushed my butt back. His other hand caressed the inside of my right leg, ever-rising until he reached my packed balls and cupped them in his palm from behind. His lips still feathered kisses over the small of my back, but he soon bit the waistband of my boxer-briefs and peeled them over my round, firm butt. The strap dragged the rest until it folded under my cheeks, Sawyer's thumb hooking the fabric in place.

Sawyer released my cock and moved both hands to my butt, pulling my cheeks to the side and leaning in. His hot breath was a welcome sensation on my tender skin. And when his lips met the core of me, I felt prickles rise all the way to the back of my head. The left side of my face pressed hard against the door, the smoothed wood caressing my skin whenever the intensity of Sawyer's movement rocked me.

Sawyer buried his face between my cheeks, his lips and tongue working my tight hole mercilessly. He wet and licked me, both hands on my cheeks now, massaging and spreading them to give him space to move. He was careless and messy, his saliva pouring plentifully and his tongue reaching from my taint all over my hole and up, slicking me for his cock.

The pressure of his hands on my cheeks was such that I shuddered all over and reached back, clasping his head and pushing it harder against myself. He rimmed me sloppily, ravaging me with his face and spit and breath.

"Fuck, please," I whimpered, not entirely sure what I was pleading for. I wanted him. I wanted more of him. I wanted everything he offered, just like I had wanted it a week ago and a month ago and when we'd first crossed paths. He was the focus of all my desires. He was the fulfillment of my greatest hopes. And I wanted our souls to collide and merge when our bodies connected. I wanted that pure, unfiltered, unrestrained joy of immersion, the blinding lust, and the unity and companionship only a passionate relationship like this could provide.

Sawyer yanked my underwear down, making me yelp in surprise, and my cock sprang free of the tangled waistband. He gripped it in his right hand, stroking me firmly and steadily, all the while pushing his wicked tongue hard against my rim.

"Sawyer," I pleaded again, and my need seemed more urgent. "...want you..."

Sawyer ignored my pleas and continued to hold me, teetering on the verge of climax and despair. The two lived so close to one another, and the line separating them was simply Sawyer's mercy, his willingness to let me throw myself over the edge and take comfort in flying high. Sawyer was anything but merciful. He tightened his hold on my cock, each thrust of his hand a tease that made me throb and itch deep within, but none of his thrusts came close to helping me orgasm.

My mouth gaped open as air flowed in and out of my lungs. My eyes rolled back, and I rose on my toes. When my soul returned to my body after the brief extra-dimensional trip Sawyer's naughty tongue had sent it on, I heard myself moaning out loud.

Sawyer pulled back from me, and I shivered. My cock throbbed dryly in the absence of his hand and cool air met the wetness between my cheeks. And when Sawyer's hands fell onto my cheeks, the slapping sound startled me more than the warm, buzzing sensation. "I could do this all day," Sawyer rasped, catching his breath.

I fucking couldn't. Suspended in this torment that tickled my pleasure with grand promises, I could only appreciate the journey after reaching its end. And my love knew it.

As I heard shuffling and movement, I kicked my sneakers off and stepped out of my pants and underwear. In the meantime, Sawyer had taken off most of his clothes, standing in his boxer-briefs, looking at me expectantly.

I was more than glad to make his wishes come true. As I turned to face him, I descended to my knees, my eyes locked onto his. His inked torso, arms, and neck were like a canvas to contemporary line art and broody, bad-boy statements, none of which he took too seriously. He was a growly one when someone looked my way, but so was I when they lusted after my keeper. I scanned his wiry torso, the definition of his pecs and abs, and the rising and falling of his chest as he breathed deeply. And I crawled a little closer until my face rested against the hard bulge that stretched his underwear thin.

My eyes darted back to his just as he narrowed them, one of his hands settling on the back of my head and the other swiping his underwear down, but not over his cock. His thickness remained hidden even as I opened my mouth wide and closed my lips over his covered tip. The soft scent of soap he'd used in the locker room shower overpowered the faint scent of his musk.

I exhaled, my hot breath washing over the bare skin above his cock just as he pulled the waistband over the tip and let me suck him in. The flavor of his precum coated my tongue as he filled my mouth and pushed deeper into my throat. It only took a minute for my throat to relax, and then I swung my head back and forth, taking him deeper with each move.

He loved to push the limits, and I loved to be tested. When his cock slid deeper in, forcing me to hold it in my throat and stop breathing, to choke on it until saliva trickled out of my mouth, I felt that I was the hardest ever. I didn't dare touch myself as a choked noise erupted from me and over his length. I didn't dare touch myself even when he pulled himself out, letting me breathe. Even the lightest caress of my length would make me explode as I heaved air into my lungs.

"Good boy," he whispered. I glanced up at his heated face, my eyelashes batting against the tears in my eyes. They were a reflex and nothing more, but they made me look sexy to him, and I knew it.

I licked my lips and opened my mouth for him again, taking him deeper and deeper until he buried himself balls-deep in my mouth and throat, all his muscles trembling, his fingers running through my floppy hair.

I forced myself to remain still, but the instincts of my body were fighting the force of my will. I grabbed his hips and held him inside of me just like that, his cock lodged in my throat, and oxygen just a distant wish. My abs tensed and trembled, and my feet thrashed. Finally, he pushed me back and pulled out, a string of saliva stretching from the swollen head of his cock to my chin.

I wiped myself with the back of my hand while Sawyer dropped to his knees. He pressed his lips against mine and kissed me softly, soothing whatever ache he imagined he'd placed on me. There were none. My heart thundered with pride that I could please him better than anyone, and my body burned for the pleasure he could offer me in return. That he did. His right hand moved from my upper back, traced my spine, and slid between my cheeks. I was still wet when Sawyer pressed his index finger against my hole, and I forced myself to relax and embrace him. My abs tensed as I pushed lightly, making myself just loose enough for his finger. And when he entered me, I neither flinched nor clenched. I embraced him. Quite literally, I tugged his hips closer to me. We kept kissing, but his hips swung back and forth, our cocks trapped between our bodies and all the while, he probed me gently with one finger.

I exhaled as he bit my lower lip and pulled it back, our eyes flicking open seemingly at the same time. He smirked, his teeth still holding my lip in a gentle, tingling bite. Then, he released it, and I murmured, "Fuck me, Sawyer."

As if some invisible force pushed us, we toppled onto the soft carpet covering most of the hardwood floor in my room. I lay on my back, legs spreading and coiling around Sawyer's waist as he laid down on top of me. He wiggled down just enough for his cock to settle itself along my taint, his abs pressing against my cock and stomach. Each contact made me shiver, but I enjoyed this tender torture as much as I enjoyed a breath of fresh air or a hot shower after a hard day. Hell, I enjoyed it more than that. It was like a hot chocolate on the first day of snow. It was like Christmas, but sinfully aflame.

Everything Sawyer made me feel was unique to him. And it was so much more than my wildest expectations that I never, even in sheer curiosity, wished to know what others felt like in Sawyer's position. He was not just enough, but the perfection sculpted to my exact shape and size.

And when he held himself in a strong grip and searched for my entrance with the tip of his cock, I released a shuddering sigh of pleasure, pulling myself up to make it easier for us both. He leaned in, his cock pressing hard against my hole, and waited for a nod from me.

Feeling his bare length on my skin was even better than before when we'd used protection. Since we'd gone exclusive and resorted to PrEP, the sensation seemed to be infinitely more intimate. He was mine in all the ways, just as I was his.

The nod he waited for came easily. There was never any doubt about that.

And Sawyer sank into me with careful moves, probing me and watching my face for any sign of wincing. When he found none, he pushed himself deeper, crossing the first inch and filling me with the next.

My breath hitched, and he jerked back, letting the pulse of pain melt into warmth, then tried again. It took me a few heartbeats to adjust to the sensation, as always, but when I did, not a sliver of pain remained. The feeling was something inexplicable. It was indescribable. Words could never do it justice. There was an element of fearful anticipation to it, suspending me in expectation of a searing bolt of pain that never came. And, as seconds ticked away, even that anticipation dissipated. In its place, an explosion of new and unique feelings sparked to life. My heart drummed with joy, drowning out all the other sounds, and warm tingling spread through my body. But it was when I set my hands on Sawyer's hips and nudged him to reach deeper into me that the true and fascinating feelings occurred. The head of his cock rubbed against the place of my pleasure, and everything in me was suddenly alert. Neediness filled me like an abstract itch I couldn't physically reach.

The back of my head rubbed against the carpet. My eyes rolled for a moment before I focused on Sawyer's blissful expression. My chest shivered as my boyfriend's pace intensified, and the slow probing morphed into ramming and slamming. He filled me deeper and harder, fucking my brains out in every sense of the phrase and shattering my world once again. Each time, he broke me into pieces and put me back together, giving me new discoveries in the pleasures of our bodies.

I was not silent. Not for a long time. Freely, I let myself moan and spill profanities that were meant for his ears only. Calling myself names for him, urging him to do me harder or love me fiercer or go in deeper. Then, when the sensation was so intense that my mind was spinning, I begged him to slow down and keep the pace just so, rubbing against my prostate at a slow, sensual pace that seemed to make the tips of my fingers tingle and my toes curl.

"Faster, please," I begged again, seeking my needs. "Please, I'm...so...close."

Sawyer gripped my throat with both hands and gazed into my eyes, leaning in so close that the locks of his hair fell down and tickled my face, his nose nearly touching mine. Sweat covered us both, and his dripped slowly onto me as he impaled me harder and faster, kicking moans and cries out of me.

The constant stimulation held me at the very edge of my orgasm, never pushing me over but never giving me a moment of rest. I grabbed the back of his head and slammed his lips against mine, a moan bursting out of me and into his mouth in an instant. I used my other hand to hold my itching, pained cock and gave it the gentlest rub that sent me over the edge.

It was as explosive as ever, my teeth sinking into Sawyer's lower lip. My cock throbbed rapidly, my hole clenched with it, and the constant pounding of his body against mine sent sputters of hot wetness splashing between our torsos.

Sawyer growled, leaning deeper in and fucking me just the same against the rapid tightening of my hole around the base of his cock. And when I felt him throb in me, white light spiderwebbed across my vision. We were so united and inseparable, his cock filling me down to the last fraction of an inch, throbbing, spilling cum into me, and I tightened around him until his eyebrows rose in painful amusement.

He let out a strained chuckle. "Fuck, Noah, that feels…oh, fucking amazing."

I exhaled and heaved for a breath of fresh air, looking into his eyes until his cock calmed and the height of the sensation passed through me. We blinked, the dim lights making sweat glisten on Sawyer's handsome face. His brown eyes caught a twinkle of the lamplight as we shared a smile that began shyly but grew and grew.

"I love you, baby boy," he whispered.

"I love you, too," I said earnestly.

He moved, sliding out of me, and I longed to feel him in there again. His absence was only soothed when he kissed me, hopped up, and extended his hand. I grabbed it, and he helped me up, then led me straight to my bed. Neither of us cared that we were sweaty and covered in the mess of my climax. Not just yet. We would care about that in a minute. For now, I surrendered myself to his love. It blazed like a wildfire. It was a tornado that swept everything into its massive whirlpool. It was anything and everything all at once.

We lay on our sides, Sawyer behind me, his body folding to fit every bend in me. His cock, softer but not yet entirely down, nestled between my cheeks, and his chin pinned between my shoulder blades so that he could kiss the back of my neck. We lay there, silent, catching our breaths, and let the heat of our bodies rise as our hearts calmed.

And as we lay there, my thoughts whirled through time and space. We had a little place of our own. Sawyer got his representation and I discovered the immeasurable joy of teaching. We upgraded to a larger place and we traveled. His fame grew and my students thrived.

We were happy.

And the rest of our lives began.

The End

Author's Note

I'm so glad you've read *Scoring the Keeper* all the way to the end. Noah and Sawyer were so much fun!

If you enjoyed *Scoring the Keeper*, I would appreciate an Amazon or GoodReads review. They are priceless to indies like me and help readers decide whether to give this book a chance.

If you'd like to give me a shoutout on the internet, you can find me in all the usual places. Just look for Hayden Hall and you'll find me everywhere online.

If you enjoy college romances, I've got two complete series available on Amazon (and free with Kindle Unlimited). You can start with *Frat Brats of Santa Barbara*.

If you would like early access, work-in-progress chapters, exclusive merch, bonus scene, and more, consider supporting me on Patreon: patreon.com/HaydenHall

And finally, if you would like to receive a free full-length novel (and sign up for a monthly magazine and book updates), you can do that here: https://BookHip.com/NDGCCQR

Love,
Hayden

Arctic Titans of Northwood U

Crossing Blades

Scoring the Keeper

Big Stick Energy

Acknowledgments

I would just like to direct your attention to a small and dedicated group of people who make this whole thing possible.

Sabrina Hutchinson deserves all the thanks and the world for the work she puts into each and every one of my novels. We started this tango in July of 2021 with *The Two Stars Collision,* and we never paused for breath.

Angela Haddon is the creative force behind these gorgeous covers. Since meeting Angela, I've been sitting on the edge of my seat in expectations for the next one, and the next one, and the one after that.

To my Patrons on Patreon, I love you. You're making a huge difference in my professional life, and your support touches my heart.

Everyone who's ever engaged with my stories, thank you. Your likes, comments, KU borrows, and purchases go a long way in helping me do what I love doing.

And finally, Xander, my love, wins the cake. He's the one who needs to live with me when I daydream about boys kissing boys, giggling to myself, and chugging the fourth gallon of coffee for the day.

Also by Hayden Hall

Destined to Fail

Destructive Relations

Shameless Affairs

Explicit Transactions

Frat Brats of Santa Barbara

The Fake Boyfriends Debacle

The Royal Roommate Disaster

The Wrong Twin Dilemma

The Bitter Rivals Fiasco

The Accidental Honeymoon Catastrophe

The Bedroom Coach Contract

The Office Nemesis Calamity

College Boys of New Haven

The Nerd Jock Conundrum

The Three Hearts Equation

The Two Stars Collision

The No Strings Theory

The Geeky Jock Paradox

Standalones

Rescued: A Hurt Comfort Novel

Damaged: A Black Diamond Novel

About the Author

Gay. Sweet. Steamy.

Hayden Hall writes MM romance novels. He is a boyfriend, a globetrotter, and an avid romance reader.

Hayden's mission is to author a catalog of captivating and steamy MM romance novels which gather a devoted community around the Happily Ever Afters.

His stories are sweet with just the right amount of naughty.

You can find out more and get in touch with Hayden through his website at www.haydenhallwrites.com or one of the links below.

Printed in Great Britain
by Amazon